'What were you afraid of, Grace?'

She swallowed hard. It was her chance to tell him about the way she'd once felt about him and the way she'd felt when they'd just gone their separate ways after that one incredible night.

'Of winding up alone and lonely,' she said. 'I think maybe I blew my one big chance. I took door number one instead of having the courage to wait for the big prize.'

'We're just different, you and I.'

'Yes. We are. It's a good thing we never got together. Isn't it?"

'I don't know.'

'You don't?' Her chest tightened.

'Who knows what would have happened if things had gone differently?'

She forced a laugh. 'Yeah, maybe we would have got married and had two-point-four kids.'

'Yeah…maybe.' He put a hand out and touched her cheek. 'I've got to go now.'

He turned and began walking away.

Grace watched, feeling oddly bereft.

Then he stopped.

And came back to her…

Available in August 2003 from Silhouette Special Edition

Drive Me Wild

ELIZABETH HARBISON

SILHOUETTE®
SPECIAL EDITION™

*Silhouette, Silhouette Special Edition and Colophon are
registered trademarks of Harlequin Books S.A., used under licence.*

*First published in Great Britain 2003
Silhouette Books, Eton House, 18-24 Paradise Road,
Richmond, Surrey TW9 1SR*

© Elizabeth Harbison 2002

ISBN 0 373 24476 2

23-0803

*Printed and bound in Spain
by Litografia Rosés S.A., Barcelona*

ELIZABETH HARBISON

has been an avid reader for as long as she can remember. After devouring the Nancy Drew and Trixie Belden series in school, she moved on to the suspense of Mary Stewart, Dorothy Eden and Daphne du Maurier, just to name a few. From there it was a natural progression to writing, although early efforts have been securely hidden away in the back of a closet.

After authoring three cookery books, Elizabeth turned her hand to writing romances and hasn't looked back. Elizabeth lives in Maryland with her husband, John, daughter Mary Paige, and son Jack, as well as two dogs, Bailey and Zuzu. She loves to hear from readers, and you can write to her c/o Box 1636, Germantown, MD 20875, USA.

This book is dedicated to Meg Ruley who, upon hearing that I had to drive the bus for my daughter's school, saw the humour I thought was distinctly lacking in the situation and said, 'You have to write it!'

Heartfelt things to Ray Plummer of Butler Montessori School in Darnestown, Maryland, who managed to keep a straight face while teaching me everything I needed to know to pass the CDL test and get on the road.

Chapter One

"You ever had to eat a locust?"

For a moment, Grace Bowes—standing in the blazing-hot sun looking for a mailbox that *should* have been on the corner of Main and Sycamore but wasn't—didn't think the question was directed at her. But when it was repeated with more vehemence, she looked toward the speaker and saw a bent old man perched on a bench in front of the Blue Moon Bay Pharmacy, staring at her so expectantly she couldn't help but laugh.

"No, I haven't." She'd never been one to believe in omens, but when the seventeen-year locusts returned to her hometown the same month she—after a fifteen-year absence—did, she had to rethink her position. On several things. "But I haven't ruled it out."

The man laughed heartily, revealing a mouth full of holes plus one or two brown stubs of teeth. "Smart girl." He thumped a gnarled finger against his temple.

"Have you?" She noticed he had a battered hat at his feet with a handwritten sign that said *Thank You* in an uncertain hand, and an old dented and rusted Partridge Family lunch box by his side. She immediately regretted asking. Maybe that lunch box was full of locusts right now.

"Had to, during the war. Would've starved otherwise." He looked her over with a sharp blue eye. "What war are you fighting?"

Divorce. Betrayal. Single motherhood. The modern job market as it related to a woman whose only real job had consisted of working as a secretary for her father, the local judge, ten hours a week one summer. A lot of wars. "I'm just looking for a mailbox. I thought there was one on this corner." She had to mail a car payment on a car that was the main asset she'd won in the divorce after her husband, Michael, had left her a note on the bathroom counter, saying he was sorry but their life together hadn't worked out and he'd found someone else.

"Used to be one right there." The old man gestured, then shook his head as if something very sad had happened. "Not there anymore."

"No, it's not." Grace glanced at her watch. In ten minutes she had an appointment at the Bayside Jobs employment agency. First she had to mail this payment, hoping to avoid at least one early-morning call mispronouncing her name and threatening unspeakable actions if she didn't get the car payment in on time. Along with winning the car, she'd won the car payment, thanks to Michael's savvy at hiding his financial assets.

Michael Bowes. He'd been the golden boy of Blue Moon Bay, Maryland, the captain of the football team and homecoming king to Grace's homecoming queen. He'd gone to college in the north and she'd followed a year later. Four years after that, they were married and Michael, then a commercial real-estate developer, had ridden a ride of prosperity right into a lovely upper-middle-class lifestyle. When the bottom had dropped out of that market, he didn't bother to mention to Grace that they were living on credit cards and line of credit advances and a host of bad gambles.

By the time he left—no doubt because thugs with stub noses and barrel chests were threatening to break his kneecaps—he'd accrued hundreds of thousands of dollars in liability. He and Grace had had to sell the house and her jewelry and even her clothes. Her yard sales were legendary. And exhausting. When it was all over, she had nothing except bad memories of a man who had once seemed like the Catch of Blue Moon Bay.

She wasn't sorry the marriage was over. Often she'd felt as if in their life together they'd lacked understanding of each other, and even real interest in each other. Perhaps if Michael hadn't made the first move, she would have suggested it herself after Jimmy was grown. She'd never know, because Michael had beaten her to the punch.

So she'd packed up their ten-year-old son, Jimmy, and moved back to her hometown to live with her widowed mother in the house she'd grown up in. It was only for a year, she told herself. She'd save enough money to move back north, so Jimmy could be near his friends again, in the town that was his home. And she could be far away from this claustrophobic hamlet.

In the meantime, she'd just get a job here in Blue Moon Bay. Granted, at thirty-three, she should be head--

ing her own household, not lying on the same bed she had as a teenager, counting the same fading roses on the wallpaper, but here she was. She was lucky to have the benefit of her mother's generosity.

With any luck it would keep her from having to eat locusts.

"You have something to mail?" the old man asked, holding out a shaking hand.

Grace automatically pulled her purse in closer to her body. Too many years in the city. "No, thanks. I was just trying to orient myself."

"Used to be a mailbox there." He dissolved into a long, sputtering cough. "Gone now."

She tried to smile and took out one of the only two dollars she had in her purse. "Thanks so much for your help," she said, dropping the bill into the hat. She noticed there were only three pennies and a nickel in there and, with a pang of pity for the old man, dropped her other dollar in too. "I really appreciate it."

"God bless you," he called as Grace walked away and rounded the corner. "And God bless your family too."

"I hope so," she whispered.

She looked at her watch again and quickened her pace, hurrying down the shaded street that ran parallel to the old boardwalk a block up. In fifteen years, almost nothing had changed. The salty smell of the ocean still hung in the air and mingled with sweet taffy and caramel corn, though whether the smell was actually there or just a memory, Grace couldn't say, since it was early May and most of the shops hadn't opened for the season yet. The pavement was littered here and there with the familiar old Hasher's French Fries bags, malt vinegar stains dotting the same logo they'd had for at least three decades. It was one of the only landmarks left, now that the once-charming holiday town had fallen in favor of the more exciting Ocean City forty-five minutes away.

Still, a few dings and whistles of arcade games echoed through narrow alleyways full of shops that only opened during the summer when the tourists came to the beach. Grace fought a feeling of melancholy. Around every kite shop, T-shirt shop, and junk-food joint were ghostly memories of bike spills, melting ice cream on muggy summer nights and first kisses in the shadows of doorways and brightly striped awnings.

She stopped at the address she'd written for Bayside Jobs and looked around. It took her a moment to realize 32 Maple Street was the tiny space that used to sell funnel cakes and, for a couple of years in the seventies, had been a head shop.

She paused outside the door and pulled the fabric of her blouse away from her damp underarms. It was a little tight, she'd noticed, thanks to her Oreo therapy, but it would probably be okay as long as she didn't raise her arms and split the back. If she stood straight, it looked fine. She hoped.

With a quick breath, she heaved the old glass door open and stepped into the cool, dark, mercifully locust-free office. It still carried the faintest whiff of grease, sugar and marijuana.

An unpleasantly familiar stout woman looked up from the desk a few feet in front of her. ''Grace Perigon,'' she said flatly, her face pink under her now-white hair.

''Ms. Lindon?'' Grace gasped, recognizing the voice that addressed her by her maiden name. Ms. Lindon— she'd always emphasized the *Ms.,* leading to rampant speculation among the students about her sexuality—had been the meanest home ec teacher on the east coast, maybe even the meanest in the whole United States.

Students had called her "the Egg Beater" because she'd always seemed hostile, even when baking a cake.

Grace felt the blood drain from her face and pool in the toes of her new discount-store pumps. "I have an appointment."

"I don't have any appointment down here for you."

"You're in charge here?" Grace glanced around to make sure, once again, that she'd opened the correct door and not, say, an acupuncturist's or a martial arts studio. "Bayside Jobs?"

Ms. Lindon's brow lowered further than was aesthetically pleasing. "I *am* Bayside Jobs."

That was it. Grace was done for. Except that she couldn't allow herself the luxury of being done for. She walked slowly toward the large metal desk. The air conditioner hissed in the corner. "Then I must have an appointment with you," Grace said, in as warm a voice as she could muster.

For a moment, she toyed with the idea of running back outside to take her chances with the locusts.

The older woman took out a vinyl-covered appointment book and studied it intently. "I don't see you here."

"Oh." This was as very bad start. "When I called, I used my married name. I'll still be using it now, even though we've gotten divorced."

"What is it?"

"Oh, just the usual, I guess. We grew apart—"

"The name," Ms. Lindon barked. "What is the name?"

She knew damn well that Grace had married Michael Bowes. Everyone did. There were no secrets in this sardine can of a town. But even if she didn't know the name, there weren't enough unemployed people in Blue Moon Bay during the summer to fill two lines of the daybook, much less an entire day, so she could have figured it out. For Pete's sake, Grace could *see* it was all right there on the page, with just a little doodle of a dog in the corner and some scribbling around the middle of the page. And her name under 11:00—Grace Bowes.

Ms. Lindon looked too long at the page before tapping the scribbled line in the middle and saying, "There it is. You were supposed to be here at eleven, not ten past. Rule number one, *Always* be on time. Bayside Girls are always *professional.*"

Bayside Girls? A pang of dread reverberated in the depths of Grace's heart. It was still 1952 here in Blue Moon Bay, just as it had always been. This was going to be hard to get used to after all those years up north.

She took a deep breath and remembered Jimmy. "Of course. I'm sorry."

"Have a seat." The Egg Beater gestured and waited for Grace to obey, then took out a pen and steno pad that still had the bargain-store price tag stuck to the front. "Now, tell me about your skills."

Grace thought she was prepared for that question. "Let's see, I've spent the past nine years chairing the annual Bingham Industrialists Golf Tournament." The pen remained poised over the pad but did not touch it, Grace noticed. "I also organized and edited the Bingham Junior League cookbook in 1996, 1997 and 1999."

After a painful pause, Ms. Lindon said, "I mean,

what kind of *marketable* qualifications do you have? How fast can you type?''

Grace smiled brilliantly. ''Typing isn't really my strong suit....''

Ms. Lindon looked at her with flat eyes. ''Computer skills?''

Grace wondered if her old Atari Pong game qualified. ''None to speak of but—''

Ms. Lindon dropped her pen and leaned back in her chair, appraising Grace with a cool eye. ''I'm afraid we don't have anything that suits your particular...expertise.''

The blood that had drained moments earlier began to rise in Grace's face. ''I'm willing to learn,'' she said, trying to keep the desperate edge out of her voice.

Something in the older woman seemed to soften. She picked up a large portfolio marked Positions to Fill in a handwriting Grace remembered from her old report cards—*Grace needs to learn that she has to work for her grades instead of expecting everything to be handed to her on a silver platter*—and leafed through it.

She shook her head. ''Mmm. No, it's as I thought. All of these jobs require the latest computer skills and good typing speed, not to mention experience. Wait— here's one that will train you—'' She squinted and looked closer. ''Oh, no. That's no good.'' She clopped the book shut. ''I'm sorry. I don't have anything for you now. Maybe if you take a secretarial class and come back, we can help you at a later time.''

Grace refused to give up so easily, even though half of her wanted to concede. ''You just said there was one that didn't require experience.''

Ms. Lindon smirked. "No, that was definitely not for you."

Grace leaned forward in her seat. "Ms. Lindon, I really, *really* need a job. *Any* job." She hated to beg the help of a woman who clearly wouldn't share a canteen of water with Grace even if her clothes burst into flames, but she had no choice. "I'm broke."

The other woman shifted uncomfortably in her seat. "I am sorry for your misfortune, but—"

"I don't want your pity." Grace swallowed hard. "I'm not here asking for favors. I have a ten-year-old son to take care of now. I need the work. Please, Ms. Lindon—" she reached out and touched the older woman's hand "—*please* tell me what you have."

A long moment passed, during which Grace wondered if Ms. Lindon would let that tennis ball fall in her court or if she'd just lob it back at Grace by the sheer force of impatience. "All right," she said at last. "But I don't think you're going to like it."

Grace tried to keep calm. "What have you got?"

"It's at Connor Primary Day School. You know, over on Bayshore Drive?"

Grace nodded, feeling a dull ache grow rapidly in her chest. Dread. Another shoe was going to drop any minute, she knew it, and it would be a size-fourteen stiletto. "I went to school there."

Ms. Lindon gave her a look of slight skepticism but didn't say anything. "Well. You may be able to work tuition for your kid into the deal if you get the job. There's one perk anyway."

That didn't sound so bad. She'd kind of like Jimmy to go to the same school she went to, if only briefly "Really? So what do they need?" She tried to imagine what job Ms. Lindon thought Grace wouldn't like.

"Playground assistant?" she asked, to let the other woman know she was willing to take that kind of job. "After-school care?"

"Bus driver."

Grace felt as if she'd missed the bottom step of a very steep staircase and fallen flat on her face. "I beg your pardon?"

"They need a bus driver."

That was it, the other shoe she'd been waiting for. There was a moment's silence while the news bounced around the room and into Grace's consciousness.

"If you're willing to do it, I can call and set up an interview."

"But a *bus driver?*" Grace was still back at square one. Visions of meaty tattooed arms and screaming kids came to mind. "But I don't know anything about driving a bus."

Ms. Lindon shrugged. "It says here that they'll train the right person."

Grace shifted her weight in her seat, which had suddenly become extremely uncomfortable. "Are you sure there's nothing else?"

"Nothing." She pushed the book aside. "You're clearly not suited for that kind of position, though."

"But—"

"I'll tell you what. I'll keep a special eye out for anything that might work for you and I'll call you immediately if I see something." She started to stand up.

"Wait." Grace put a hand up. "How much does it pay? The bus-driver position, I mean."

Ms. Lindon looked in the book and quoted a figure.

Grace did some quick calculations and said, "That could work. I could survive on that pay." She'd carefully budgeted what she needed to save each month in order to be able to move back north in one year. This salary would cover that and leave a little over at the end of the month for incidentals. It would be a strenuously budgeted life, but it would be temporary. "I'll take it."

"That's only if they hire you, of course."

There was that knot in the pit of her stomach again. "Do you think they won't?"

"I don't suppose you've ever driven a bus before?"

"No." *Of course not.*

The older woman shrugged. "Might not matter. It does say they'll train. You'd have to interview first, of course. I can only refer you. Whether or not they hire you depends on how that interview goes." She hesitated before adding, "If you really want to try it."

"I do." Grace took a slow breath. She wasn't going to get sidetracked into a discussion about whether or not she knew what she was saying. "You mentioned there's a tuition benefit for my son?"

"Says so here. You can talk to Mr. Stewart about that more if you interview."

Grace noticed that *if.* "Okay, set up an interview." She straightened and brushed a fly off the front of her dove-gray Armani suit. She'd bought it in Milan two years ago. Things were different then. "I'll be a bus driver."

Chapter Two

The familiarity of the Connor Primary Day School campus was disconcerting to Grace. It was as if nothing had changed in the twenty-some years since she'd attended, except that the trees were a little taller and the buildings looked a little smaller. Hope mingled with melancholy as she parked the car and got out to walk to the old red barn where the garage was located. Was it merely familiarity that was making Grace's stomach flutter this way, or was it a premonition that she would get the job and everything would—eventually—be all right?

Having always been an optimist, she decided to believe the latter.

The office door was shut when she reached it, and for one terrible moment she feared that Ms. Lindon had sent her on a wild-goose chase. Grace had been so insistent about interviewing for the job that maybe the woman had just sent her out here to get rid of her. Her fear was exacerbated when she knocked and there was no answer. Within a few seconds, she'd almost convinced herself that there wasn't even anyone here when a movement behind the old mottled-glass door caught her eye. Someone *was* here. Ms. Lindon wasn't *that* mean—Grace had just let her imagination get carried away. She took a quick breath to bolster her nerve and knocked again, more firmly. A voice called out something inside, but she couldn't understand what it said. Come on in? Or maybe Go away! Or even Get help, fast, I'm being held at gunpoint!

Now what was she supposed to do?

Deciding it was better to go forward with confidence than to appear timid, she opened the door and poked her head in, surprised to find she was so blinded by the sun outside that she couldn't see in the dark, cool office. "Mr. Stewart?"

"That's right. What can I do for you?" The man's voice was nice. Smooth and kind, and she felt herself relax when it reached her.

She stepped in from the heat and said, in the general direction of the voice, since her eyes hadn't yet adjusted to the light, "I have an appointment to interview with you. About the job opening here."

There was an uncomfortable moment of silence while the splotchy figure across the room sat unmoving. Just as he was beginning to come into view, he said, in a voice she was suddenly able to place with absolute clarity, "Grace?"

Her stomach dropped. She imagined it plunking on the ground next to her and bouncing like an india-rubber ball. She blinked hard, and within a few seconds her vision came back to normal.

She almost wished it hadn't.

There, before her, was a face she'd envisioned a million times over the years, a face she'd never thought she'd see again. A little older, of course, but the same golden tanned skin, now with a faint web of lines around the clear blue eyes. Same dark wavy hair that, in contrast, had always made those eyes absolutely striking. She'd always reacted physically to them, and to the charismatic man they belonged to.

Luke Stewart.

Grace couldn't have been more surprised to see him if he'd been lassoing steer in her mother's backyard. God almighty, she'd never *dreamed* Luke was the Mr. Stewart she was supposed to see. She didn't even know he was still in town. Not only in town, but here, not ten feet away from her, behind a desk that was piled with papers, the odd piece of horse tack and quite possibly control of her future.

It seemed like twenty minutes that Grace stood there, trying to recapture her breath and find a voice beneath the stomach and heart that had lodged themselves in her throat. It wasn't merely surprising to see Luke, it was deeply disconcerting. It had always been disconcerting to be around Luke Stewart, but why hadn't she outgrown this particularly juvenile kind of heart-pounding, lip-trembling, struck-dumb reaction?

Just because once upon a time, a long time ago, she'd thought she'd loved him.

But instead of telling him, she'd married his best friend.

It was Luke who finally broke the silence. "You're back."

She nodded. "For a while."

He held her gaze. She felt as powerless as a mortal

in a Greek myth, unable to look away. "I thought you were gone for good," he said.

Grace hoped she could sound calm and unaffected while her insides raged. "You just never know about people," she said pointedly.

"No," he agreed, just as pointedly. "No, you don't." He took a deep breath and blew it out, shuffling papers on the desk. "So. How long are you planning to stay?"

"About a year. I want to take my son back to New Jersey as soon as I can. To his friends and his school and all."

Something flickered across Luke's expression, but it was gone before she could identify it. "I heard about Michael. I'm sorry."

Had he heard it from Michael himself? Surely not. They'd been pals in high school, but as far as Grace knew, they hadn't spoken in years. "I really don't want to talk about it."

He shrugged. "Never did. What are you here to talk about, Grace?"

"I'm here about school business, of course."

"Of course. How old's your boy?"

"Ten." Grace tried to think of something else to say, but she was stymied. She began to be aware of perspiration trickling down the center of her back, and wondered if it was the unusual May heat or this conversation with Luke that caused it.

She was completely over him.

Had been for years.

All of which was for the best, since he had never shared her feelings. In fact, during the three years of high school when they'd seen each other the most, they'd spent about 90 percent of their time arguing.

"So you're looking to enroll him here for the year." Luke nodded as if he'd figured out a puzzle. "We should probably move this discussion to my office and start over."

"This isn't your office?"

He looked around at the mess. "No. This is the garage. You wanted the main building. It's just lucky I happened to be here."

Lucky wasn't the word that came to Grace's mind. "This is where I was told to come," she said, feeling her face grow warm and hating herself for it.

"Someone told you to come to the *garage?*"

She sighed. "Look, Luke, I'm not here to enroll my son and volunteer for classroom cookie duty, I'm here about the job. So are you going to interview me or not?"

"The *job?*" he repeated, as if the idea were incomprehensible. "What job?" Though his manner didn't show it, he must have been rattled, because she'd already said why she was here. "There's only one job opening here, and that can't be…driving the bus?"

"Yes." Grace raised her chin defiantly. "That's the job I'm here about."

He laughed. *Laughed!* "Give me a break."

"What?"

"Come on. You're Junior League, not bush league. You can't be serious."

"I'm completely serious." Then she added, under her breath, "How many times am I going to have to say *that* today?"

A year ago, Grace couldn't possibly have envisioned herself *begging* to be a bus driver. Someone could have won a lot of money on this bet.

He studied her for a moment, then said, "I don't believe it."

"What, do you think this is a joke? Do you think I just blew into town and decided the first thing I had to do was track you down, take some abuse about my marriage, then pretend to beg you for work? Does that make more sense, Luke, than Bayside Jobs sending me here looking for legitimate employment?"

"Actually, I have a hard time envisioning either scenario. But if Mary did send you here to drive the bus, I can't even imagine what she was thinking. I'm afraid she had you come out here for nothing."

"Mary?" Who was Mary?

He turned and looked at her sharply, as though he'd caught her trying to making faces at him. "Mary Lindon. You did say you were sent from Bayside."

"Y-yes." *Mary?* Lord, Grace must have called her *Ms.* Lindon forty times today and the woman hadn't once stopped her and said, as almost anyone else would have, "Call me Mary, please." Grace cleared her throat. "Mary thought I'd be perfect for the job."

"Really," he said, but his tone said *bull.*

Grace nodded. She had to compose herself, had to return the tone of this meeting to something less personal, more professional. "Obviously this is a little awkward, since we know each other. Is there someone else I should speak to instead?"

"Someone higher up, you mean?"

"Well…"

"I'm the headmaster," he said, flatly. "I'm afraid it's up to me."

Headmaster? Oh perfect—she'd really blown it then. "Okay. Well, I came here for an interview, like anyone else off the street, so pretend I'm a stranger." She drew herself up. "Now, are you going to interview me or not?"

A muscle ticked in his jaw for a moment, before he said, "Sure. If that's what you want." He jotted her name on the back of a telephone book on the desk and drew a line under it, then looked at her, obviously trying not to smile. "Tell me how long you've been driving school buses now, Grace."

Heat rose in her cheeks. He wasn't going to make this easy. "The job description clearly said that no experience was necessary."

"Maybe not *necessary,* but it helps. More qualified drivers will have the edge there." He made a note of it. "You have a commercial driver's license?"

She heard a single minor piano chord ring ominously in her brain. "Oh, come on, Luke, what do you think?"

He leaned back in his chair and gave her a lazy look that would once have made her toes curl, but now just ticked her off. "I think you're applying for a job driving a bus, so you must have at least some vague notion of what that job entails."

She tried to stay calm. "I think it entails starting the engine and driving from place to place picking up children and bringing them to school, which is pretty much what we, in my old neighborhood, called 'car pooling.' How different can it be?"

"For one thing, you need a commercial driver's license in order to do it here."

"I can get one, right?"

He gave a half shrug that said *wrong.* "Have you learned your way around an engine since I last saw you?" he asked. By now his face wore the same bored expectation of a negative response that an airline clerk had asking if you'd packed your own suitcase.

This was no time to give up, Grace reminded herself, however tempting that might be. "I can learn."

He released the pencil, letting it clatter to the desk. Then he leaned back, took a deep breath and let it out slowly, not unlike a hissing bus tire that had just run over the sharp shards of her broken heart. "Grace, I ask you this in all seriousness—do you have any idea what's involved in taking this job?"

She straightened in her seat and smoothed her jacket, instantly regretting the prissy gesture. As a prospective bus driver, she should have brought a toothpick to chew on or something. "Not entirely."

"For the license test, you'll need to know the bus's engine inside-out. They're going to pop the hood and have you identify and locate every part of the engine, then they're going to have you get down on your knees and identify the parts from underneath." He counted his points triumphantly on his fingers. "*Then* they're going to ask you what happens if any of those parts fail or wear out, and they're going to ask you how to fix them." He gave a small but meaningful shake of his head. "If you pass all that, then you get to take the driving test."

It did sound daunting, but not as daunting as another registered letter from the IRS. "And you're saying you don't think I can do that?"

"I can't see it, no." Clearly he was harboring his old hostility toward her. "Point is," he went on, "I'm expecting to hire someone who already has."

"What if you *can't* hire someone who already has?" she asked. "What if no one like that applies?"

"They will."

"When do you need a driver?"

"For summer school. In four weeks."

"Four weeks!" She threw up her hands. "And you're only looking to hire someone *now?*"

"You're not helping your case."

"I'm trying to help *yours. And* mine." She could tell she was getting nowhere with him. She remembered a chocolate bar for Jimmy that she'd put in her purse earlier, and made a mental note to inhale it the second this miserable meeting ended. "Look, maybe I should talk with someone else about the job, since you obviously can't be objective about me."

"As a matter of fact, I'm in the unique position of understanding just how wrong you are for this position." He sighed and softened his voice. "Grace, you'd be miserable. Why are you even here?"

"Because I *need* work," she said, trying to keep her voice steady. "And this is the only possibility in town."

"But it's *not* a possibility."

"It *is.*" She knew she sounded desperate, but she didn't care. She *was* desperate! "You can teach me whatever it is I need to know, and I can take the test and do the job so quietly you won't even have to think about it again. I might be the best damn bus driver you ever had."

"And you might hate it and quit after two days."

"I won't. I promise."

"Well, you've already said you're leaving town next year. I'm not hiring a lifeguard for the summer, I need a bus driver. I need someone who's going to take the job, do it well and keep it for more than a single school year." His gaze grew penetrating. "This is nothing personal."

"Yes, it is!" She jabbed a finger in the air at him. "Personal is *exactly* what it is. You're obviously holding something against me from a hundred years ago—''

"Not true."

''—but if you think it's easy for me to sit here and beg you for a job, you're mistaken. If *I* can get past our history enough to work together, surely *you* can.''

"We don't have a history."

"Of course we have a history! We've known each other for eighteen years.'' A small hurt flared in her, like a match lit on a windy night. How could he act as if they were total strangers? Maybe they hadn't always gotten along, but once or twice in their past Grace had gotten the feeling that they had connected on a very deep level.

One instance in particular came to mind.

But now it was as if he was so eager to distance himself from her that he would even go so far as to distance himself from the facts. So she decided to remind him of those facts. "We went to high school together, Luke. You were my husband's best friend, for Pete's sake. That's history."

"That," he agreed, "is history."

She hesitated, unsure as to whether he was agreeing with her about the whole concept or if he was making the point that his friendship with Michael was history, as in kaput.

Because she knew that.

She remembered when it had happened.

Before she could think of something to say, Luke spoke again. "It's irrelevant whether we have a history or not, because this is about qualifications. And you don't have them. At least not the right ones."

"I'll bet I have better qualifications than most people you interview for this job," she argued. "Have most of your applicants taken the Red Cross CPR course for infants and children? Can most of your applicants arbitrate an argument between two ten-year-olds? Can any of your other applicants tell the difference between the Robo-Crusier-Insect-Man and the Auto-Alien Transformer?''

Luke raised an eyebrow. ''You think being able to make that distinction will come in handy?''

Her gaze was direct and serious. ''You just never know.''

He studied her quietly for a moment, then, with a small nod, he said, ''That's true. But it doesn't change my mind.''

''What would?'' she asked plaintively.

He took a deep breath. A deep *dismissive* breath. ''Look, I've got to admire your determination, but I don't see this as a good fit. So I'll keep your number on file and—''

''And what?''

He sighed. ''And hope you forget this whole idea.''

''I can't afford to,'' she said, quietly but firmly. ''I need this.''

''You're not half prepared even to take the test, and like I said, summer school begins in just four weeks.''

''But I can learn, like *I* said.'' She raised her chin and challenged him. ''Besides, you're ignoring some rather obvious extenuating circumstances.''

''Am I?''

Grace gathered her energy. ''I won't pretend to be able to read your mind, Luke, but I know you well enough to tell when you're cornered.''

He raised an eyebrow.

She continued, ''*You* need a driver. As you yourself have just pointed out, there are only a few short weeks until school starts, and—'' she looked around the room ''—I don't see a lot of people lining up for this position, no matter how optimistic you may be about that happening as soon as I leave. *I* need a job. And while I may not have the exact qualifications you're looking for, I'm willing to learn whatever I need to in order to satisfy your requirements. It seems obvious to me what you need to do.''

There was a long silence during which she trembled under his familiar gaze.

Finally, Luke broke the silence.

''You're absolutely right. It's very clear what I have to do.''

Hope surged in her. ''Good.''

Luke stood up and gave her a cool appraisal. ''Thanks for coming by, Grace. I'm sorry this didn't work out, but good luck finding something else. And welcome home.''

Chapter Three

Luke stared at the closed door in disbelief.

Grace Perigon.

No, make that Grace *Bowes,* trophy wife of his high-school partner in crime—it was hard to call Michael a *friend*—and the only girl who'd ever really gotten under his skin.

Even now, with the perspective of so many years, it was hard for him to say just *why* she'd gotten under his skin. Sometimes he'd thought he'd hated her. Other times…well, other times, he'd thought maybe it was the opposite.

One time—one short, stupid night—he'd been *sure* it was the opposite.

But that had passed quickly. And in the end, he'd watched her leave town without looking back while he, all in all, had to say he was glad to see her go. As Michael had pointed out to him, not so subtly, he didn't have what she was looking for in a guy: money, position and the potential for rapid advancement.

Not that he'd ever let Michael, or anyone else, know of his feelings for Grace.

Michael had just seemed to pick up on the situation himself. It wasn't that Michael was particularly perceptive, or so spiritually bonded to Grace that he perceived anything extraordinary about *her,* it was only that he always believed everyone wanted what he had. And he was ace at keeping what was his, whether it was a car or a girl.

Michael Bowes had somehow even managed to get Blue Moon High School to retire his football jersey at the end of his unremarkable varsity run.

The strange thing was that Luke had never known Michael to let go of any of his prized possessions, even after he'd completely lost interest in them. Once in high school Luke had spotted a broken Louisville Slugger in the back of Michael's garage when they were working on his vintage '65 Mustang convertible...and Grace was a much finer prize than that Louisville Slugger.

It was hard to imagine Michael letting go of *her.* Luke had been surprised about it ever since he'd heard the news several months back that they were divorcing. At first he'd half expected Grace to come back to town, but when she hadn't come right away, he figured she never would. He'd figured he was safe.

He'd figured wrong.

Turned down for a job as a bus driver.

That was bad enough, but she'd been turned down by Luke Stewart, who she never thought she'd have to see again...much less under circumstances like these.

She'd made a mistake with Luke, there was no doubt about it. A mistake, it seemed, he'd never forget. Or forgive. She'd made a bad bargain for her future, and, in the process, wounded his male pride. It was nothing more than a glancing blow to his ego, but he was still willing to use it against her, even under circumstances as dire as those she faced now.

Her life couldn't get a lot worse than this, Grace thought, kicking a dead locust from the path in front of her and feeling mean. She was living at her mother's again, with no money and no skills to get a job, even a lousy job. That was another bad bargain she'd made: the housewife bargain. Believing her future to be secure, if not deliriously happy, she'd concentrated her efforts on making a comfortable home for her family. In so doing, she'd let technology and the job market pass her by. Now she could barely even see them in the distance.

So much for saving for her future.

It was beginning to seem entirely possible that she'd be stuck in this sandpit of a town for the rest of her life. She'd become one of those wacky old ladies whom everyone referred to as "Miz Grace." Except for the kids who would call her *dis*-Grace, and who would ring her doorbell late at night and run.

She walked across the pretty green campus and thought ruefully of how nice it would have been for Jimmy to go to school here, just like she had done herself. Blue Moon Bay was a far cry from Morris, New Jersey. Here you could see horses from the school room window instead of traffic. Jimmy would love that.

When she got to the small gravel parking lot, she noticed a familiar older man getting out of a shining Lincoln. It only took her a moment to place him.

"Mr. Bailey?" Fred Bailey had been a friend of her parents for years. A lifetime bachelor, he was a big lawyer with offices in D.C. and Annapolis. He'd lived in Blue Moon Bay since he was a young man. In fact, he'd grown up with her mother, and gone to school with her through twelfth grade. They'd even dated briefly before he'd gone off to law school at Princeton.

He'd moved back to Blue Moon Bay six years later, after Grace's parents had married, and made the 90-minute commute to his offices, remaining a pillar of Blue Moon Bay society. Though Grace hadn't thought about Fred Bailey in a very long time, seeing him brought back a flood of warm memories. He was so much like her father that she had to fight an impulse to run into his arms. She could imagine how he would smell, of peppermint and pipe smoke. Just thinking about it made her feel more relaxed than she had for months.

"Mr. Bailey," she said again.

He turned to her, his expression blank.

Her heart sank.

"It's Grace Bowes...Perigon," she said, fighting back a sudden overwhelming weakness in her limbs.

His face broke into a wide smile. "*Grace?* Good heavens, I wasn't expecting to see you here!" He patted his breast pocket and took out a glasses case. As soon as he put his spectacles on, his eyes grew wide behind the thick glass. "So it *is* you!" He opened his arms, and she gave him a hug. "Welcome home, child. I've been looking forward to seeing you ever since I heard you were coming back. How long has it been?"

"Since Dad's funeral."

"My goodness, that's a long time. Look at you, just as lovely as ever. Your father would be so proud." He smiled again and clucked his tongue against his teeth. "I still miss the old fellow."

She smiled, and her chest felt full but her eyes burned again. "Me too."

"Well, what are you doing here?" Fred Bailey asked. "Not coming back to school, I expect." He chuckled.

"Apparently not," she said, a touch wryly.

"Beg pardon?"

She shrugged. "Well, I was here to apply for a job, but apparently I'm not properly qualified." She resisted the childish urge to say, *That mean, spiteful Luke Stewart wouldn't give it to me.*

Mr. Bailey's brow lowered. "What job? I didn't think there were any teaching positions open."

Grace cleared her throat lightly. "It wasn't a teaching job."

"Not teaching?" He wasn't going to let this go. "Was it administrative?"

"It was driving. The bus. Driving the school bus." There. She'd said it. She'd admitted out loud that she'd been turned down as a bus driver.

It felt even worse now.

"Driving the school bus?" the older man repeated, with the same incredulity he might have shown if she'd said she wanted to become a trapeze artist. "That's no job for a Perigon. Let's go talk to Luke Stewart and see if we can't find something reasonable for you here." He took her arm and started leading her to the building she'd just left.

"No. Please." Her reaction was too strong. He dropped her arm, startled. She smiled. "I mean, the driving position really was the one I wanted. It had flexible hours and would allow me to be with Jimmy when there was no school." She tried to imagine Luke's reaction if she reappeared with a big gun like Fred Bailey, demanding that a new position of some kind be created for her. "But it doesn't matter, because he doesn't think I'll be able to get the license on time." She didn't know why she felt like she had to defend Luke's decision suddenly.

"Hmm." He rubbed his chin. "Well, I must confess I don't know much about that."

"It's okay. I appreciate your concern, but I'll find something else."

"I'm sure you will." Mr. Bailey looked at his watch. "I must go. I've gotten so caught up in talking to you, I forgot I had a board meeting. I want to see more of you now. Welcome back, Gracie."

The endearment took the edge off her anger toward Luke. Nobody had called her Gracie since her father had died.

"Thanks, Mr. Bailey." The lump in her throat expanded like a sponge. It was silly to feel a melancholy nostalgia for her childhood, but she did. She watched Fred Bailey walk away, noticing his gait was now that of an old man, a little creaky, stiff in the knees. It was then that she really realized that home *hadn't* just waited for her, unchanging, while she went off and started a new life up north. Things had moved on here, too. People had died, grown older; some had moved away years ago, never to be seen again.

Thomas Wolfe was right, Grace thought, you can't go home again.

But sometimes you have to.

"You'll find something," Grace's mother, Dot Perigon, said, patting her daughter's shoulder sympathetically. "If you like, I could speak to some of your father's old friends and colleagues. They all loved Daddy so much, I'm sure at least one of them could find something for you to do."

Grace shook her head and fiddled with a sweating glass of iced tea her mother had put on the table in front of her. There was a twist of lemon and a mint leaf in it, just the way she had always made it. "I'm desperate, but not so desperate that I'm willing to take a job at someone else's expense. It's one thing when there's a job that *needs* to be filled—" she thought angrily of Luke "—but quite another when someone just creates a position as a favor to an old friend, then has to pay for it."

"But anyone would be lucky to have you around, helping out."

"Only if they needed the help, Mom. And I think most of Daddy's friends have got highly qualified personnel working in their offices already."

Dot sighed and topped Grace's glass off with tea from a pitcher. "All right, dear, but I'd be glad to speak with Fred Bailey. Or anyone else," she hastened to add. "If you change your mind."

Grace smiled. "Actually, I spoke with Mr. Bailey today."

Dot looked surprised. "You did?"

"Yes, he was on his way to the school when I was leaving."

"What did he say?" Dot asked sharply.

Grace was afraid she heard, in her mother's voice, a determination to speak with her old friend on Grace's behalf. And Grace definitely didn't want that. "As a matter of fact, he did offer to twist some arms for me," she said, deflecting the idea she hoped, before it could take root. "But I told him no thanks."

"You did?"

"I had to," Grace stressed. "I don't want charity."

"I understand. Still, it was very nice of him to offer." Dot looked quite pleased. "Very nice."

"Yes, it was." Grace took a long draw of the cold tea. "You know, it was almost like having Daddy around for a moment. When I saw him, it brought all of that back to me."

"I know what you mean," Dot mused, with a small smile.

"So you've known him since high school, right? Mr. Bailey, I mean."

"Yes, why?"

Grace stirred her tea thoughtfully. "I was just wondering why he never got married." But she was really thinking, again, of Luke. How come *he* hadn't gotten married? Was he going to end up like Mr. Bailey, a lifelong bachelor in Blue Moon Bay?

"I couldn't say," Dot answered, looking out the window. "Looks like Jimmy's having a good time with the Bonds' old spaniel out there."

Grace took a cookie off the plate her mother had set out. "He loves dogs."

"Maybe you should get him one."

"Mom! I can barely take care of the two of us as it is, despite Michael's meager monthly payments." It was then that it truly hit her. She had to take care of herself and her son, and if things continued the way they were, she wasn't going to be able to. She'd have to…she didn't even know what she'd have to do. Go on welfare? She shuddered at the thought. "What if I could find a job as a cocktail waitress or something over in Ocean City? Do you think you could keep Jimmy at night?''

Dot frowned. ''I don't want to say no to you, honey, but…well, I sometimes have things to do in the evenings. I just can't commit to staying home according to your schedule.'' She assumed a pleasant expression and added, ''But, as I told you, he's welcome to stay with me any time during the day.''

Grace swallowed her shock. Though she wouldn't say she'd ever been spoiled, exactly, and she'd always been careful not to take advantage of her mother, at the same time she never thought her mother would say no to her. Especially on something as important as this.

But Grace was well aware that Dot had already been very generous in letting her daughter and grandson move in with her. Grace wasn't going to argue for more. ''Do we still have today's newspaper?'' she asked, trying to sound upbeat, although she felt anything but. ''Maybe there's something there that I overlooked before.''

Right. Like a classified ad offering a miracle to the most desperate candidate. Now there, Grace thought wryly, was a position she definitely was qualified for. High qualified.

''So what's she doing at night that she can't reschedule?'' Jenna Perkins asked Grace a few nights later. After an unproductive week of job-hunting, Grace had reached the end of her rope. She *had* to get out. Now she and Jenna were in a crowded downtown bar called Harley's, shouting to each other over the throbbing beat of a terrible band. Jenna was Grace's oldest friend and had once shared Grace's dream of leaving Blue Moon Bay, but she had stayed when the time came to decide.

In reflection, it seemed like the better choice. She'd married a carpenter and had twins two years after Grace had Jimmy.

"Think she's got a secret life you don't know about?" Jenna went on, then raised an eyebrow. "Maybe a boyfriend?"

Grace laughed. "I don't think so. Can you imagine it? Mom *dating?* Good lord!" She shook her head and reached for the peanuts. "Like life hasn't gotten weird enough as it is."

"Ten years is a long time to be alone," Jenna said lightly. "And your mom's a very attractive woman."

"Come off it, Jenna. She's known everyone in this town for sixty-three years. I don't think anyone new has come in to sweep her off her feet."

Jenna shrugged. "You never know."

"You said you had a great job idea," Grace reminded her, steering the conversation away from her mother. "What is it?"

"Well, you know how I was working in my dad's shop last month when he and Mom went on that cruise?"

"Sure, I remember." Jenna's father was the only jeweler in Blue Moon Bay, and his shop had been there since his own father had established it in the forties. "What do you have in mind? Knocking off a jewelry shop and pawning the stuff at your dad's?" Grace laughed.

Jenna laughed with her. "Don't think I haven't thought of it. But no, there was a woman who came in like three times while I was working, and she must have spent at least three grand just on big tacky rings and things. Know what she does for a living?"

"What?"

"She reads tarot cards."

Grace groaned. "Oh, no, you want to be a fortune teller?"

"Wait a minute, I've been thinking about this for a while now. I think I could make a mint off the summer tourists. Probably even enough to keep us going the rest of the year, if that woman is any indication. Although she did say she works in Atlantic City, which, granted, has a bit more tourist traffic. But still, I might be able to make a living off it."

"Right. You, Bob and the twins, all living off the telling of nineteen people's fortunes." Grace shook her head. "I don't think so."

"There are more tourists in Blue Moon Bay than that and you know it. The town's going to be mobbed in a couple of weeks, just you wait."

"Mobbed by Blue Moon Bay standards, anyway." Since leaving town, Grace had seen "mobbed" on a grand scale. Atlantic City in summer. Walt Disney World in summer. Blue Moon Bay did get a fair amount of tourists and beach-goers, but its reputation as a family-beach town kept the wild singles and college kids away. They went to Ocean City, forty miles from here, for their fun, leaving Blue Moon Bay comparatively quiet. "But it's not like it's going to be mobbed with the kind of people who go to fortune tellers."

"*Everyone* likes fortune tellers. You should do it too," Jenna went on, unperturbed. "Say thirty bucks a reading, two readings an hour, ten hours a day, six days a week, that's…" She paused, thinking.

"Unlikely?" Grace supplied.

She shot Grace a look. "Thirty-six hundred bucks a week, right? With virtually no overhead. I could live with that.'' She shifted on her barstool, nearly slipping off. The bartender approached and she shouted an order to him, then turned back to Grace and said, ''Now where was I?''

''Dreaming.''

''No.'' Jenna speared an olive from the bartender's supply with a toothpick, then popped it into her mouth. ''Tarot cards. Seriously, think about it.''

''How about if you try it and let me know how it works out. In the meantime, I'm going to find a *real* job.''

''Well, you haven't so far. I would think you'd be willing to at least *consider* some untraditional alternative possibilities.''

''You'd be surprised at some of the untraditional alternatives I've thought of.'' Grace took a swig of the Mexican beer Jenna had ordered for her, but the lime slice got caught in the neck of the bottle. She poked it down and tried again, appreciating the cold, sour taste. Michael would never have come to Harley's bar and had bottled beer with fruit in it. He'd always preferred the muted cocktail scene at the Seahorse by the bay.

Somehow the fact that her ex-husband wouldn't like it here made the beer taste even better.

''I hate to ask this,'' Jenna started carefully, ''but have you thought of borrowing money from your mom?''

Grace shook her head. ''Dad's pension is good, but not so good she that she can support Jimmy and me.'' She sighed. ''Besides, then I'd be in debt to her, and I'd have to make the money to pay her back, so what's the difference?''

''All right, but I wish you could just stay here indefinitely. If only there was a job.''

Grace shook her head. "You can't go back home."

"But you *are* back home."

"It doesn't feel like it." In truth, *nothing* felt like home at the moment. Grace felt completely and utterly lost.

She leaned back against the bar and let her eyes fall on the people playing pool across the room. The music of the band pounded through her, and she willed it to shake loose the tension that had become a constant hum inside her head. She had to take at least an hour or two off from worrying, or she was going to have a nervous breakdown. There was nothing she had to think about right now, she told herself, nothing she had to take care of right this moment. Jimmy was home with Jenna's husband and kids, and there was nothing Grace could do about her job situation tonight. This was a great opportunity to loosen up, and she was going to enjoy it, no matter how hard it was.

As if testing her resolve on that cue, the band started playing "Stand By Your Man."

Jenna clucked her tongue against her teeth. "They've got to be joking."

"No, God is." No sooner were the words out of her mouth, than the glass door to Harley's opened and Luke Stewart strolled in. "Uh-oh. Time to leave." She set her bottle down and hopped off the barstool.

"What?" Jenna asked, looking in the area of the door. "What's wrong?"

"That's wrong." Grace said in a low voice, pointing to Luke.

"Oh, my God, it's *Luke Stewart*," Jenna gasped. "You haven't talked to him since high school, have you?"

"As a matter of fact, I talked to him a few days ago.

I had to beg him for a job driving a bus at Connor School, and he turned me down.''

Jenna looked at her, surprised. "You had to ask Luke? Why? Is he in charge of the buses?''

"He's in charge of everything," Grace said, popping an olive into her mouth. "Headmaster.''

"Oh, my. That must have been hard. How come you didn't tell me earlier?''

Grace chewed and kept narrowed eyes on Luke. The sight of him brought a warm flush to her cheeks. Residual humiliation and anger, no doubt. "If you'd been turned down as a bus driver, you probably wouldn't be talking about it much either.''

"Wow. I guess he's still mad about you picking Michael over him.''

"I didn't pick Michael over him. I stayed with Michael rather than throw the relationship away over a small, brief, untested crush on someone else.''

"On Luke, you mean." Jenna pulled the bowl of peanuts across the bar and took a handful.

Grace kept her eyes on Luke. "It doesn't matter who it was, it would have been stupid for me to throw away a secure relationship because of some silly infatuation.''

"I don't know. It might have spared you a lot of trouble.''

"And bought me a whole new brand of trouble.''

Jenna nodded her agreement. "Probably so. And you wouldn't have Jimmy.''

"That's right. He's worth it all." Grace sighed. "Too bad he's going to have to live on bread and water because his mother can't get a job, even as a bus driver.''

"Well, why would you want to drive a bus anyway?

And why there? Wouldn't it be weird to go back to your alma mater that way?''

Of course it would be weird. It felt weird even before she knew Luke was part of the deal. ''There's no other work in this town,'' Grace said dully.

''Oh, come on, I'm sure someone would hire you. One of your dad's old friends? You know, as a favor to him?''

Grace winced inwardly. ''I'd sooner die than shame Daddy by taking charity from one of his friends. They'd feel obligated, I'd feel pathetic…it would be the same as asking for a handout.''

Jenna shook her head. ''You're just as stubborn as you've always been.''

''I'm not stubborn, I'm *mature*.'' She laughed. ''Besides, if I worked for the school, I could negotiate tuition for Jimmy into the deal, and we'd keep exactly the same hours.''

''That makes sense. And it *is* a good school,'' Jenna acknowledged with a sympathetic smile. ''Jimmy'd like the horses.''

''That's what I thought. But it's not like I have the option of taking the job.''

''Well, there are minuses to it too. This is probably for the best.''

''Unemployment, in this case, is *not* for the best.''

''Surely there's *something* else you can do that would fit the bill. *Some*where.''

Across the room, Luke had stopped and was talking to a petite blonde with a heart-shaped butt and a waist the size of Grace's thigh. Drawing her attention away from the two, Grace pulled the bowl of peanuts over and took some. To hell with fat grams. ''Yes, I'm sure. I'll find something else,'' she said, still watching Luke with a growing constriction in her chest. Nerves. But the anxiety she was trying to escape continued to escalate. Her breath stopped when she noticed Luke glance in her direction, but he didn't seem to see her.

Jenna followed her gaze and asked, "So why did he turn you down?"

"I'm not sure." She'd remembered he was great-looking, of course, but she hadn't remembered just how great-looking he was. The jerk. "I believe he thinks I'm not clever enough to pass the test and then drive the big, bad bus," Grace said, taking a last sip of beer. Part of her was actually reluctant to leave, but she didn't trust herself to be entirely civil to Luke if he should see her. "And if *I* screwed up after *he'd* hired me, he'd look really bad in front of the board."

Suddenly, Luke turned and walked purposefully in her direction. It felt as though all the noise and music and people receded into the background. Grace was as acutely aware of him as she would have been if he were following her down a dark alley with a ski mask on.

Before she could turn away and pretend she hadn't seen him, he raised a hand in greeting, and she had no choice but to do the same.

"The usual," he called.

"Sorry?" Grace said, at the same time hearing a voice behind her say, "You got it, Luke," over the din of the band and the crowd around them.

Oh, God, he wasn't even talking to her. He'd been waving at someone behind her, and she'd waved right on back at him, like a fool. Would this day never end?

He walked right past her without acknowledgment. Then he stopped and stood behind her at the bar, apparently oblivious to her presence. He wasn't more than two feet away from her back. She could feel the heat of him, penetrating the thin fabric of her shirt.

She slipped some money out of her purse and whispered to Jenna, "Pay the bill and meet me outside." She had to get away before he did notice her.

"Grace?" Too late. It was Luke's voice. He'd spotted her.

She turned with as much cool as she could muster. "Oh. Hey, Luke. Did you hire someone for that job from the hundreds of people I saw lined up by the garage when I was leaving?"

He didn't play along. "I left a message on your answering machine." His voice was clipped. The bartender handed him a bottle of beer with no glass. He took a gulp of it, then let out a short breath. "You get it?"

"A message?" Grace was mystified.

His eyes, which had seemed such a warm shade of brown earlier, were hard. "You got the job." His mouth turned up in the smallest ironic smile. "Surprise."

Grace caught her breath. She was employed? *Really?* This was too good to be true—or was it? "I don't understand. The other day you told me I didn't."

He took another draw off his drink and set it down, hard, on the bar. Foam bubbled out of the top and ran over onto the gleaming wood bar. "I've been outvoted."

Her excitement turned to apprehension. He was angry about something. Had Mr. Bailey said something to him after all? "What do you mean you've been outvoted?" she asked cautiously.

He lowered his chin fractionally and gave her a look that could, under the right circumstances, have been extremely sexy, but which was, instead, downright accusatory.

Something cold slithered down her spine.

"I mean," he said, with too much patience, "that starting in three short weeks, it'll be your job to sit on a seat covered with chewed gum, in a vehicle equipped with a Bodily Fluid Clean-up Kit, surrounded by screaming kids. Just like you wanted." One side of his mouth cocked into a smile. "This must be a dream come true for you."

His iciness left little doubt that Fred Bailey had indeed leaned on him.

"I applied for that job without help from anyone," she said defensively.

"And I turned you down without help from anyone." He drank, then leveled his eyes on Grace. "If it had stopped there, we'd have no problem."

"What happened?"

"Fred Bailey happened," he said, confirming her fears. "He strongly 'suggested' that I reconsider you for the position, no matter how unqualified you are. What did you do, call him from your cell phone as soon as you got outside?"

"No!" Grace was hurt by the accusation. "I saw him in the parking lot when I left, and he asked what I was doing there. When I told him what happened, he offered to talk to you, but I declined. I had no idea he'd done it anyway, and I'm sorry he did."

"This is the way things have always worked for you, Grace." Luke shook his head and took an angry slug of his beer, hammering it back down on the countertop.

"And just what is *that* supposed to mean?"

"That means it's always been easy for you. You've always known just what you wanted and gotten it." He lowered his voice slightly and added, "No matter what the cost."

She railed in anger. "That's not true. Number one, if you think this is my dream job and I went after it pulling all the powerful strings I could because I wanted it so badly, you're crazy. And number two, I would hardly say my life is easy. You have a lot of nerve making presumptions of any sort about me." She caught her breath. "And what do you mean 'no matter what the cost'?"

He looked as though he was about to fire back at her, then stopped. "That's none of my business. It's between you and whoever you make your deals with. I shouldn't have said anything."

"That's right, you shouldn't. You have no right to judge me, Luke Stewart. No right at all."

"I'll keep my thoughts to myself from now on."

"Right," she said. "Like you always have, huh? Like you even *can.* You may not *say* anything, but you have a way of getting your disapproval across."

"I don't think you want to have that conversation," Luke said, in a voice that assured her that she did not.

"I don't want to have *any* conversation with you!"

He raised an eyebrow. "Then you're going to find it particularly tedious to work for me, don't you think?"

She threw her hands up in the air. "So what do you want me to do? You want me to say I won't take the job?" she asked, fighting the urge to do just that. "You want me to quit before I even start?"

He gave a quick shake of the head. "Oh, no, I don't want you to quit. I want you to come in tomorrow at

7:00 a.m. and start learning the parts of the engine.'' He gave a quick, humorless smile. ''You had your chance to decline. Now you have to go through with this. We need a driver and, like it or not, you're it.''

Chapter Four

Three weeks later, Grace knew more about school buses than she'd ever dreamed she would. It was Wednesday, two days before she was set to take the test for her commercial driver's license and five days before the first day of summer school—when she was supposed to begin driving.

Assuming she passed the test, that was.

It apparently had a first-time failure rate of 49 percent. Grace would have accepted those odds more comfortably if she hadn't already come out on the short end of the 47-percent failure rate of first marriages.

She and Luke stood before the bus in the early-morning heat. It was not yet nine o'clock. Luke had insisted that Grace meet him on campus every day at 7:00 a.m. so they could get their work done before it got too hot and humid outside. Or so he said. She suspected the early hour was really because he wanted to make this whole experience as miserable as possible for her.

"All right," Luke said, taking a sip of steaming coffee from a paper gas-station cup. "The test official is going to ask you to go through an outside sight inspection first, identifying all the major parts of the engine and frame."

"How can you drink steamy coffee on a hot morning like this?" Grace asked. "You know, they make whipped frozen coffees that are really good."

He gave her a look. "Is it necessary to discuss my drink preferences, or can we just move forward with what's actually important?"

"Okay, okay. Move on." She took a deep breath, like an athlete preparing for a sprint. "I'm ready."

He stepped back and gestured toward the bus. "Then go for it. Tell me everything you're checking as you do it."

"Okay." Her hands tingled with nervousness, but she wasn't about to admit to him that this was harder than she thought it would be. If he noticed her shake, she'd blame it on the frozen whipped coffee she'd had on her way in. "First I check the headlights, taillights and brake lights, to make sure there are no cracks." She walked around the bus, looking at all the plastic covers on the lights as she spoke, then stopped where she'd started again. "Everything looks fine."

"Everything?" he asked, as if he'd caught her in a lie.

"Oh, the reflectors." She'd nearly forgotten the reflectors again. For some reason she had made that mistake almost every time. She made another round, then came back and looked to Luke for approval.

He said nothing, just watched her impassively.

She wasn't going to let him rattle her. "Okay, then. Tires."

"What about them?" His mouth almost lifted into a smile. Almost.

She couldn't help but admire the curve of his lips. That was something she'd always noticed whenever she saw him. He had a great mouth. Not full and girlish, but not lipless and hard. Just right.

And, she remembered with a reluctant shiver, he'd known just how to use it.

"Tires?" he prompted. "What are you supposed to look for there?"

She shook herself back into the moment. Tires. "The tread has to be four thirty-seconds of an inch, the rims have to be rust-free and smooth. No cracks. Valve caps on. And you can't just take them off another car in the parking lot like you could with a normal car."

"Is this the kind of thing you're planning to say to the cop who tests you?"

She ignored his question and turned to kneel in front of the first tire. She half suspected Luke might have changed it since she went through this drill yesterday, but it looked the same. "So now I'm supposed to take the hubcap off—" she wrestled with it until it came free "—and check the slugs and grease seal."

"Lugs," Luke said.

"Huh?"

"It's *lugs.* You keep saying slugs." For the first time in two weeks he smiled. "You're talking about tires, not guns."

"I said lugs," she lied, disarmed by his grin. What a weapon he had there. "You heard wrong."

"Uh-huh." He could see right through her.

She'd always been a terrible liar. "Where was I?"

"You mentioned tread, rims, valve caps, grease seals and 'slugs,'" Luke said. There was a light in his eyes for a moment, but it dimmed quickly and he was back to business. "Anything else?"

Obviously he had something in mind. What was she forgetting now? She repeated the list in her mind twice before it came to her. "Air! I'm checking the air pressure. And making sure there's no fabric showing through the rubber tire. Although, frankly, isn't this the kind of thing they check for you at the gas station when you go to full service?"

"You're not going to full service anymore, Grace," Luke said. "At least not on the school's dime."

He was right—she wasn't living in a full-service world anymore. Not here *or* at home. She went back to her drill, checking each tire in turn. "Next I check the wiper blades, the gas door," she moved from one part to the next as she spoke, "and the running board." She stepped on it and pushed hard with her foot. The bus rocked.

What would Michael say if he knew she could identify a running board?

"What are you checking for?"

She was ready with the answer. "To make sure it's secured tightly."

"Good."

This was high praise from Luke. She gave a nod of acknowledgment, her mood lightening. "Now, Mr. Tester, if you wouldn't mind helping me, I need to make sure the lights are working properly."

"This isn't a magic show, Grace," Luke said. Or, rather, growled. "You've got to take this seriously."

He wasn't going to allow her even a moment of levity, Grace realized. And he certainly wasn't going to let her act as if they were friends. This was all business, nothing more.

She was lucky he didn't insist she call him "sir."

"Forgive me," she said, stopping just short of rolling her eyes. "But you said I'm supposed to have a second person, in this case the MVA guy looks at the lights while I turn them on and off."

"That's right. Just don't get cute."

"God forbid."

"Well, I know that's gotten you through a lot of things in life—"

"Oh, yeah, I've been cruising on cute for years now, Luke. It worked wonders with the mortgage holder when Michael left." She put her hands on her hips and glared at him. "Cute got me lots of clams in the bank too. This bus stuff is just a hobby for me."

He looked at her for a moment, one eyebrow raised and an expression between amusement and exasperation on his face. "You finished?"

"Are you?"

"For now." He smiled again. Twice in one day. It was a record.

She couldn't help but smile back. Which really galled her. Was she so desperate for kindness that this little morsel—even from Luke Stewart, who couldn't be called friendly, much less a friend—made her feel so grateful? "Then if I may continue…?"

He nodded.

She opened the side door, stepped into the already-hot interior of the bus and took a moment to compose herself.

She inserted the key into the ignition and called out as she flipped switches, "Taillights, brake lights." She stepped on the brake pedal, recited, "Back-up lights," then put it in reverse. "Tag lights on?"

"Yup."

"Great." She shifted back into park. "Now I have to check the engine." She located the hood latch and pulled it. Then, with false confidence, she stepped out into the sun again, moving in front of the engine.

It was a mess. She'd been over it a thousand times in the past two weeks, taken notes, even drawn a rudimentary picture of it with identifying notes, but when she looked at it with no notes or instruction, she was lost.

She could not let Luke know she was anything less than completely sure of herself. She started with the one part she could identify most easily. "First I check the battery to make sure there's no corrosion and to ensure that the cable's on tight." She did so, slowly and deliberately, while she frantically tried to collect her thoughts and figure out what was next.

He must have sensed her confusion, because, without a derisive word, he leaned over the engine, brushing his arm against hers in the process. "What's that?"

Her bare skin tingled from his touch, and Grace was disgusted with herself. New low, she noted. It had been so long since she'd been with a man that even this lightest of touches from a guy she didn't even *like* sent shivers running through her. Pheromones were blind.

She focused on the part he pointed to. "The, uh, the steering-wheel rod," she said, her voice weak.

"What about it?"

Steering-wheel rod, steering-wheel rod… A flood of information came back to her, right in the nick of time. "I have to make sure that it's secure, not loose."

"Right." He stepped back. "What else?"

She pictured the drawing she'd done. "I need to make sure the brake-fluid level is correct, and that the brake lines are tight and not leaking." She rattled the list off without looking away from the engine. She could feel Luke behind her, his eyes on her, and she knew if she turned and looked at him, she'd forget all of it.

"I'd check the power steering," she continued, pointing to various parts as she went along, "power-steering pump, water pump, carburetor, window-washing fluid." She was on a roll. "I need to check the alternator, to make sure the clamp is on securely and the wires are secured behind it. Then there's the heater hose, the coolant, the radiator hose, transmission fluid, and oil dipstick." She checked it all and turned to him triumphantly. "And that's it for the engine."

"No, it's not."

"It's not?"

She deflated like a balloon. As hard as she'd tried, as much as she'd concentrated, she'd *still* managed to forget something.

"You didn't check your belts."

Automatically her hand flew to her waist.

"In the engine."

"I know," she said, trying to look at him like he was crazy for thinking she'd had anything different in mind. She bent over the engine and tugged at the fan belt. "They shouldn't give more than an inch." She turned back to him. "Words to live by, right, Luke? Don't give an inch."

"You think I'm inflexible?"

"If the shoe fits…"

"Hey, you're here, aren't you?"

She looked at him in disbelief. "Not because of any great flexibility on your part!"

"I'm being more flexible than you think."

Something in Grace snapped. She was so sick and tired of feeling like a burden to people—to her lawyer, who was letting her pay in installments; to her mother, who was letting them live with her; to Fred Bailey, who had taken it upon himself to get this job for her; and even to Luke, who had been "persuaded" to give her the job against his will and who now had to take the time to teach her the ropes—that she sometimes thought she might just scream.

"Look, Luke," she said, with as much control as she could muster. "I *know* you don't want me here. I *know* you think I can't do this, and I know that even if you *did* think I could do it, you would resent the hell out of the fact that Fred Bailey suggested that you give me the job."

He gave a short laugh.

She continued without stopping. "I know all of that, but none of it is going to make me quit. All it's going to do is make me more determined than ever to succeed at this, so you should be glad that, whether you wanted to or not, you just hired yourself the best damn bus driver you could have gotten." The timbre of her voice rose as she spoke, and she took a moment to breathe and regain her composure. "Now. I'm going to take the test in two days and I'm going to pass it and I'm going to drive the kids to and from school, and I don't want to hear one more word about how undeserving I am—got it?"

He looked at her for a long moment, during which she doubted the wisdom of her mini-diatribe, then the wisdom of taking the job, then the wisdom of wearing

cut-off shorts that made her feel as bloated as a poi-
soned cat.

The silence went on so long that she was about to
ask if he was all right when he spoke.

"Hit your knees," he said.

Grace's mouth dropped open. *"What?"*

He gestured at the ground. "You're not finished with
the test. Hit your knees and identify the parts underneath the vehicle."

"Oh." The color came back into her cheeks.
"Okay."

"What did you think I meant?"

"Nothing," she said quickly. "I knew what you
meant. I'm supposed to check the parts underneath,
front, back and sides. I know that."

Smiling to himself, Luke watched Grace bend down
and look under the front of the bus. He couldn't help
it, he loved the way she looked in those faded blue cut-
offs. Her legs were long and shapely, and already
tanned even though it was still early in the summer.
Somehow those cut-offs reminded him of endless hot
summers, and clumsy passion and foolish optimism.

"Luke?"

He was so lost in thought that he didn't realize for
a moment she was speaking to him. "Yeah. Sorry, I
was…thinking about something."

She raised her eyebrows. "You back now? Should I
go on?"

"Absolutely, yes."

"Okay." She cleared her throat and turned back to
the bus, giving him a pretty dazzling view from behind.
"I check the stabilizer bar, guide arm, tie rod, *tie rod
ends*—" she emphasized the tie rod ends, he noticed,
since that was one of the items she consistently forgot

"—brake lines to the disc brakes in front and the drum brakes in back, coil spring, shock absorber, power-steering pump, Pitman arm." She took a breath. "Make sure there are no leaks in the power-steering box, radiator hose, fuel pump and water pump." She stood up and slapped her dirty hands against the front of her shorts. "Everything's okay from the front."

"Good." He'd barely been able to keep his mind on the engine parts, so he hoped she hadn't forgotten anything major. She got down on her hands and knees at the side and started talking again. "All right, here are the transmission lines, and they are *not* leaking. The cross beams are secure, no cracks or leaks in the mufflers—" she looked back at him "—of which there are two. If you're to be believed."

"There are two," he confirmed.

"It's just that I've never heard of a car having two mufflers," she said.

"This isn't a car, it's a bus, and there are two mufflers on it."

"Okay." She shrugged. "I've just never *heard* of it."

"But you've *seen* them," he said, exasperated. "You're supposed to be looking at them right now."

"Well, I am."

He hesitated. "Grace?"

She looked guilty. "What?"

"*Are* you looking at them? Are you looking at anything as you identify it, or are you just rattling off a bunch of stuff you memorized?"

"Does it make a difference?"

"Does it make a difference?" he repeated incredulously. "Of *course* it makes a difference!" Grace was hopeless, he decided. There was no way she was going to pass the test unless she was able to charm whoever was administering it. If it was Bob Gaylord or Stan Vanderhof she'd be okay, but if she got Myrna Franz, Grace was in real trouble. "Grace, we've spent two weeks going over this damned bus, piece by piece. I know it's not the most interesting thing you'll ever do—"

"Luke."

She spoke so quietly that he stopped.

He looked at her. "What?"

She crooked a finger at him, beckoning him over. "Come here. I'll show you."

He went to her and crouched next to her, and tried to ignore the seductive scent of her shampoo...which told him he was too close to her for his own good.

"That," she said, "is the drive line. We're checking to make sure the universal joints there—" she identified them correctly "—are secure." She swept her arm down toward the back tire. "There you have the leaf springs, held on at the spring hanger and secured, as you can see, by a U-bolt. That also holds the rear axle *there* in place."

She was right on all counts. He leaned in and looked to make sure. It was hot between them, but he wasn't sure if it was the engine, the weather or something else.

"That's the gas tank," Grace was saying. "That's the emergency-brake cable, and the oil filter is over there on the right side." She turned to him, her face just inches from his. The blue of her eyes was so clear he almost felt he could see inside her. "And this—" she gave an ironic smile and pointed at him "—is a guy who is so convinced he's right about everything and everyone that he's unwilling to give anything a chance, even when it could be to his own benefit.'' She flashed him a devious smile. ''How'm I doing?''

He had to hand it to her. Not only had she learned all of the parts of the engine—a feat he had been certain she couldn't accomplish even in a year—but she had done it in less time than it had taken the last two bus drivers.

Of course, she was wrong about him. He was nothing if not open-minded.

''You're getting there,'' he conceded, with a grudging smile.

A strange moment passed between them. For just a fraction of a moment, Luke thought that maybe he and Grace might someday, somehow, be friends.

But everything that had gone down between them came back to him in a flash. ''Friends'' seemed unlikely.

Grace's smile widened. ''I'm there, buddy, I'm finished. At least with the outside of the bus and the inside's a piece of cake. I got everything right and you know it.''

He gave a nod. ''I know it.''

''Ha!'' She stood up and wiped the dirt off her hands again. ''And you hate it,'' she said, jabbing a triumphant finger in his direction.

''No, I don't, Grace, I'm glad. I need you to get this right. I need for you to pass the test.''

She nodded. ''I'll pass.'' She swallowed visibly, but kept her chin up in a determined way. ''Don't you worry about that.''

''There you are, Grace, Luke.''

Luke turned to see Fred Bailey making his way across the gravel parking lot. ''I'm glad to find you both here. Saves me some time.''

"Hi, Mr. Bailey," Grace said, sounding like a kid.

"What's up, Fred?" Luke asked. If Fred Bailey was looking for him, he could be pretty sure it wasn't to give him a lollipop. Fred only sought him out when there was a problem. Or a woman who needed a job.

The older man took a handkerchief out of his pocket and swabbed his forehead. "Hot as hell out here."

"It is," Luke agreed.

"Bet it's worse in that tin box." Fred nodded toward the bus.

Grace laughed. "Yeah. It has no air-conditioning."

Fred seemed genuinely surprised. "No air-conditioning?"

She gestured toward the open bus door. "There's a fan rigged up to the rearview mirror, but that's it."

Luke flashed Grace an impatient look. "There's nothing wrong with the bus. On hot days, the driver can open the windows and use the fan. It's just fine in there."

Grace remained silent.

Fred Bailey looked at her quizzically, then shrugged. "You all know more about these things than I do. Tell you why I'm here.

"It's about the funding."

"Maybe I should let you two speak in private," Grace said, glancing from one to the other.

"No, no. Part of what I have to say concerns you too, Grace."

She raised her eyebrows. "O-kay…"

"Luke, I'll get right to the point. Daphne Silvers has decided not to give the school the grant she promised. It was, as you know, substantial."

Luke's stomach dropped. Substantial was right. Daphne Silvers had promised the school fifty thousand dollars. He'd worked it into the budget and *still* come up slightly short of his five-year projections. The fund-raising plans he'd made were meant to fill the leftover gap, not a chunk as large as fifty grand.

"We've held an emergency meeting of the board," Fred went on, "and we're about to have another meeting this afternoon. Bernard Hall has offered an additional ten thousand on top of the donation he made this spring, but we're still falling short."

"Far short," Luke said. "Though there's a possibility that the state will give us a grant. I've got the paperwork on my desk."

Fred shook his head. "Unfortunately, the deadline for that was yesterday."

"*What?* That's not possible. I went over every detail. I'm sure the deadline is next week."

"Typo." Fred waved his hand airily, as if to say the issue had already been raised and dismissed. "They sent out an amendment, but no one on the staff seems to have gotten it."

Which meant that he'd have to wait another ten months to apply again. The school had only enough money, assuming full enrollment, to maintain itself for two more years. If that didn't change, Connor Primary Day School would have to close.

"Why did Mrs. Silvers rescind her offer?" Grace asked.

"That's beside the point—" Luke began.

"No, no, it's a good question," Fred said. "She rescinded her offer because of our policy change on the honor code at the end of last semester."

Luke nodded miserably. He'd known some old-schoolers would disapprove of the change, but he'd felt strongly that the code, as written, wasn't fair.

"What change?" Grace wanted to know.

"There was some cheating on the final exam. About six students in Amanda Bittner's class. The old policy was that if anyone cheated, the entire class would be expelled. But that was plainly unfair." He looked at Fred Bailey. "Surely you pointed that out."

Fred nodded and swabbed his forehead again. "Several of us tried valiantly, but Daphne hates scandal. Didn't want her name attached to anything that smacks of dishonesty. And she's not the only one—she nearly got Ginger Anderson and Lynn Morrow on board with her."

"But that's so narrow-minded!" Grace objected.

Luke agreed privately, but aloud he said, "These are older folks who have been living in this town for half a century or more, Grace. Not only are their personal codes of conduct strict, but they hold almost impossibly high expectations for everyone around them."

"Exactly so," Fred agreed. "So we've got to walk the straight and narrow, Luke, the straight and narrow. We can't have anything happen this year that has even the slightest appearance of impropriety."

Luke nodded. "Absolutely."

"Mr. Bailey, you said this had something to do with me," Grace said, her voice a little smaller than usual. "I hope my presence here hasn't been the cause of any trouble, what with my divorce from Michael and all."

Luke shot a fast look at Fred. That hadn't even occurred to him. Admittedly, Luke hadn't wanted to hire Grace, but he wouldn't stand for her termination on the basis of her personal life.

Fred looked surprised. "Certainly not, my dear. It's nothing to do with your divorce. It's about your *job* here."

Grace swallowed visibly. "My job?"

The older man nodded and looked regretful. "I'm afraid so. One of the budgeting proposals before the board is to cut out transportation."

Chapter Five

Grace's stomach dropped. They might cut out transportation? As in, she might lose the only job she could get?

It was totally consistent with the year she'd had, she thought cynically. She'd lost her husband, lost her home, begged Luke Stewart to give her a job as a bus driver, and now she was going to lose even that.

Obviously—and this could not be overstated—she had really ticked off the Man Upstairs somewhere along the line.

"We can't cut out transportation," Luke said, with the merest glance her way. "People are counting on it."

The glance was not lost on Fred Bailey. He followed it to Grace, then said, "There are other jobs."

Luke hesitated a small but noticeable fraction of a moment. "*Students* are counting on it," he said.

"Some of these kids live miles away, with parents who, for whatever reason, can't drive them to school. If we lose transportation, we lose students, and that means we lose revenue."

"Tell me something, Luke. How many buses do we have here?"

"Two."

"For how many students?"

Luke thought for a moment. "About twenty-five."

Fred grimaced and swabbed his forehead again. "That's only about ten percent of the student body. Last time I looked, we weren't making much profit on transportation fees. With the cost of oil going up, we might even be working at a loss."

"No way." Luke shook his head. "We're making several hundred dollars' profit with each transportation contract we have."

Fred gave a shrug that said he wasn't quite buying it. "We'll talk about it another time," he said dismissively. "We're not making any changes immediately."

Luke expelled a tense breath and stood very rigid beside Grace. "I hope a few alternative plans were introduced."

"Of course, of course," Fred said. Grace got the impression that he'd already made up his mind about it. "Now there's just one more thing."

Grace could almost feel Luke's agitation growing.

"What's that?" he asked, clipped.

"As you may recall, the board wants the staff to be certified in CPR."

"That's right." Luke looked at Grace. "Did you say you were certified?"

"Well, I took a class at the Red Cross, but I don't have the actual certification." She was about to add that she'd signed up for a refresher class at the fire-house already, but Luke interrupted her.

"That's okay," he said. "You can just take the course here. I should have mentioned it before. It's a new policy, and I wasn't thinking about it when I hired you."

"She's not the only one who needs the certification," Fred said, raising an eyebrow at Luke.

"I know, Libby Doyle in the math department is already scheduled for a class in Dover this summer when she goes to visit her family."

"What about you?"

"Me?"

For a second, Grace felt sorry for him. She'd been to his office; she knew he had a lot piled on his desk already. Although she questioned whether they needed to work on the bus so early in the morning, she did believe that it had taken some effort on his part to carve out that hour or so he had to do it.

"The entire staff needs to be certified," Fred was saying. "My secretary already looked into it and discovered that the Red Cross is sponsoring an all-day course at the firehouse next month."

"What's the date?"

"Saturday the 20th," Grace answered. "I saw the sign at the pharmacy and thought at the time it would be a good idea to refresh my memory, so I signed up."

"Wonderful!" Fred was clearly delighted. "Such a clever girl. You are your mother's daughter." He turned back to Luke.

"So all we need to do is sign you up."

"I'll be there," Luke said, sounding as if it were the last thing on earth he wanted to do.

"Excellent," Fred said, patting his handkerchief

along the back of his neck. "Glad you're both willing to pitch in this way."

Luke nodded, as if he'd had a choice, which everyone knew he hadn't. Then he looked at his watch. "I'm sorry," he said to Grace, "but I have to get inside for a conference call in fifteen minutes, and I'm not going to be around in the morning. How about if we finish this tomorrow evening? Say, around seven?"

"It's a date," she said, automatically.

He didn't correct her, but he might as well have for the dark look he gave her. "Seven," he repeated. "We'll do one last drill. After that, you're on your own."

"*When* are we going home?"

"We *are* home," Grace said to Jimmy for what seemed like the tenth time the next day. "For now." She stabbed the ground with a trowel, thinking of Michael, and tossed the dirt aside. It was late to be planting tomatoes and basil, but she'd bought mature plants, and with a little luck she'd have a midsummer harvest. "You're going to have to think of it that way."

Jimmy rubbed his eyes with dirty hands, streaking mud across his lightly freckled face. His blond hair was sprinkled with dirt, like powdered sugar on toast. "But it's not like home."

"No." Grace tried to temper her frustration at having to make him feel better about the move when she was having so much trouble feeling good about it herself. "For one thing, you've got this nice big yard to play in."

"Yeah, and no one to play with." She didn't like the sulky edge to his voice. It sounded too familiar. She herself had said almost the same thing to her

mother last night when they were talking about the unlikely possibility of Grace ever having a date again.

*It's not like there's anyone to go out with in this
town even if I wanted to, which I don't.*

"So you'll have to get out and meet new people,"
Grace said, like a tape recording of her mother.

"There *are* no new people here."

She turned to him, startled. It was *exactly* what she'd
said, but she had reason to say it. Blue Moon Bay held
on to its inhabitants the way a spiderweb held
flies...once you were trapped here it was difficult to
leave. It was hard to say whether that was because
people loved it so much or whether it was just too
much trouble to move away. Unless, of course, one was
an attractive eligible male.

But whatever problems Grace had with moving
back, it should have been a dream town for a kid, with
the ocean and the bay and the freedom and safety of
living in a town where everyone looked out for everyone else.

"*Everyone* here is new to you," Grace said.

"Everyone here is *old!*"

Grace laughed. "Come on, you've met Jenna's
kids."

"They're *babies*. They're only, like, eight."

"Well, don't worry about it, because when you start
summer school you'll meet a bunch of new kids."

"That's another thing," Jimmy said, like a little lawyer with his Evidence Against Blue Moon Bay all lined
up. "Why do I have to go to summer school? If we
were back home, with Dad, I'd get the summer off like
normal kids. Like my friends."

Grace winced inwardly. He was absolutely 100 percent right. But if he were back home, he'd be going to

a school that was less academically challenging than Connor. "Well, in this case it's a *good* thing you have summer school, because you *will* meet kids your age there. See? So it's all working out perfectly."

"Dad's not here," Jimmy muttered, kicking a bag of topsoil.

She was tempted to point out that Dad had seldom been around in New Jersey either, that whole days had passed when he got home after Jimmy had gone to bed and was asleep in the morning when Jimmy got up for school…but pointing out Michael's parental inadequacies wouldn't really make her feel better, and it for sure wouldn't make Jimmy feel better.

Grace set her trowel down and pulled off her gardening gloves. "He's not at our old home either, honey," she said gently, putting an arm around her son's narrow shoulders. "You know that. It's not as if we could just drive back to New Jersey and walk into our old life. We're making a new life, you and me. And if we can just be a little open-minded about it, we might be able to make a really great life here. Maybe we won't even want to leave." But she couldn't imagine things turning out that way.

"I'll *always* want to leave," Jimmy vowed.

"Why?"

"Because this place is stupid."

Grace experienced an unusual twinge of protective loyalty toward her hometown. "No, it's not, Jimmy. This is where your parents grew up. It should be interesting to you for that, if for no other reason."

"Do people here hate Dad?"

The question was so unexpected that for a moment Grace couldn't formulate a response. "Why on earth would you think that?" she asked at last.

He smushed the topsoil bag with his toe, staring intently as he did so. "You do."

"I don't," she said, trying to convince herself that it wasn't a lie. "Dad and I just can't be married to each other anymore. There are lots of people I can't be married to whom I don't hate." Luke Stewart came to mind, a little joke from her subconscious.

"Does everyone know he left us?"

It broke her heart that Jimmy felt the abandonment so keenly. If Michael had a bit of heart to go with his good looks, he would have made more of an effort to maintain contact with his son. Since the divorce, though, he'd been in California seven months out of twelve and had only seen Jimmy about once a month when he was around.

"No one knows the details of what happened with Dad." Of course, everyone knew at least some version of it. She'd heard several variations on the story herself. "You know what? Most people I've seen are just so glad we're here. I can't tell you how many people have come up to me and said what a fine young man you are."

Jimmy's face reddened. "They don't know me."

"But they want to. Give them a chance, Jimmy. You might really like them."

He shrugged.

"And look at all this *room* you have." She gestured at the backyard with the trowel she had picked up again. "We didn't have a tenth of this in New Jersey. I think you're going to have a lot of fun out here this summer." She got up and went to him, pulling him into her arms. "I know it's hard, buddy. It's kind of hard for me too. But if we stick together and make the best of things, I think we might end up even happier than we were before.''

That much, at least, she believed. It was certainly possible for her to be happier divorced than she'd been with Michael. From the day they'd married, she'd felt a certain sense of *this is it?* They'd dated in high school and college and everyone had expected them to get married, so they had. They'd moved to the suburbs, bought two cars, had a child, done all the things that were expected.

If she was honest, Grace had to admit that it wasn't the stuff that fairy tales were made of. In a way, she couldn't really blame Michael for wanting something new. What she blamed him for was the way he set about getting it, and the way he'd treated his family— his *son*—in the process.

''There is one thing that might make me happy,'' Jimmy said slowly.

Grace frowned. ''What's that?''

''A dog.''

''A dog.'' Just as her mother had suggested.

She liked dogs. She'd had one herself, growing up. So why was she so resistant to the idea?

She knew why; it was because Michael was allergic, or at least he'd claimed to be, though she'd never seen him so much as sniffle. She remembered, with some irritation, how, during her teenage years, they always had to put Buff, her golden retriever, in the laundry room when Michael was coming to the house. Before now, a dog for Jimmy hadn't even been a possibility.

Now it felt as if getting a dog would be the final nail in the coffin of her marriage to Michael.

''I think it's a great idea,'' she said.

He brightened. ''Really? I can get one?''

"Are you going to take care of it? Feed it, walk it, brush it?"

"Yes!"

"Then I don't see why not." It was so good to see that hope in his eyes again. She smiled and pulled him into a hug again. "Why don't you think about what kind of dog you want, big or small, and we'll go to the humane society tomorrow and look."

"Yes!" He pumped his fist in the air. "I'm gonna have a dog!"

And we're really building a home without Michael now, Grace thought, without regret.

"Go on in and get ready to go to Jenna's now," she said to her excited son. "I've got to go back to the school for a couple of hours."

For once, he didn't argue. He skipped into the house so lightly she wouldn't have been entirely surprised to see him click his heels together. She would bet he'd clean his face and hands without being told.

She picked up her gardening tools and dropped them into a bucket by the door before stepping into the cool, air-conditioned house.

"Will you be going out tonight?" her mother asked when she walked into the kitchen to get a glass of iced tea.

"I don't think so, why?"

Was it her imagination, or did her mother blush? "I might have some company, and I wondered if you would be around."

"Company? Who?"

Her mother took a cloth and busied herself drying dishes that were already sitting, dry, in the rack by the sink. "Oh, it's not important. Just a member of my bridge club."

Grace was interested. "A *male* member of the bridge club, by any chance?"

Dot set the cloth down and looked at her daughter. "Now why on earth would you ask that?"

Grace laughed. "Because, Mom, you're acting very cryptic about this whole thing."

"I certainly am not!"

"Okay, okay. Look, do you want Jimmy and me to get out of here tonight so you can have your friend over? We could go to a movie or something."

"Grace Ann Perigon, you do not need to leave the house so I can have a friend over! I merely asked because I wanted to plan on how many pretzels to buy if I had company. But, now that I think of it, I'll probably go out to the movies myself."

Her mother was definitely hiding something, Grace thought. It was either a boyfriend, plans for a surprise party, or she had joined a cult and it was her turn to host the meeting. Assuming it wasn't the latter, Grace's birthday wasn't for two months, so it had to be a boyfriend. But why hide that?

Grace suspected she knew why. "You know, Mom, if you ever *did* want to date someone..." What could she say without sounding condescending? It wasn't her place to approve or disapprove, but she had a feeling her mother might worry that she would feel weird about it. "Well, I just think it would be a good idea."

"What would be a good idea?"

"You dating. If you met someone. Although," she added cynically, "who you could meet around this place, I don't know."

"There are lots of nice men around here, honey. You'll meet someone."

"Who said anything about *me?*" Three days earlier

Roger Logan, who had a wife and four kids, had approached her in the produce section at the supermarket and asked if she wanted to meet him for a drink later. That about summed up the options for Grace here. She wasn't even *thinking* about dating for herself.

Her mother smiled and took two glasses out of the cabinet. "This is about you, isn't it?" She went to the refrigerator and took out the pitcher of iced tea.

"What do you mean?"

Dot poured and handed a glass to Grace. "All this negativity about Blue Moon Bay? Sometimes I think you're looking for excuses not to like it here."

"Why would I do that?"

"Because it reminds you of the years you spent with Michael?"

And the years she spent before that, years in which she could have been taking a different direction with her life. "You think you're pretty smart, huh, Mom?"

Dot smiled. "It runs in the family."

Grace raised her glass to her mother, drank, then went to her room to shower before going to meet Luke. Not that she wanted to impress him; it was just that her pride prevented her from showing up filthy and giving him one more thing to dislike about her.

She stripped her clothes off in the bathroom and looked in the mirror. The strong afternoon sun had toasted her skin, leaving a white impression of her halter top behind. The light in this bathroom had always been flattering, and made her tan look deeper than it was. For a moment, she felt as though she'd time-traveled back to a summer two decades before, when she used to cover her Roxy Music album in tin foil and prop it on her chest as she lay in the sun, wearing no more protection than baby oil. She shuddered at the thought now and wondered how many of the faint lines around her eyes she could attribute to that, and how many to the stress of Michael's abrupt exit.

She took a quick, cool shower, wrapped herself in a towel and went back to her room. It was only five o'clock. There was time for her to rest for a few minutes before going out, so she lay down on the bed and stared at the faded rose wallpaper.

She remembered when her father had first put it up for her. She'd been eight and had just danced in her first ballet recital. Daddy had told her she was a real little lady now, and he let her pick out new ''grown-up'' wallpaper to replace the zoo pattern they'd put up when she was a baby.

This wallpaper had seen her through a lot. The sketched red flowers had hung there, bright but just a little melancholy, through giggly sleepovers; all-night teenage telephone conversations; delirious first dates and tearful breakups; her dog Buff's death; getting ready for her high-school prom—and her wedding day.

And if the wallpaper had absorbed anything of her thoughts over the years, it had absorbed more than a little Luke Stewart, especially during one summer when, briefly, their relationship had changed.

Grace and Luke's association had always been... heated. Throughout their high-school years, it had seemed to be the typical animosity that tended to exist between a guy's best friend and his girlfriend. They argued over almost everything, from which weekend nights were for Grace to whose fault it was when Michael came over at 3:00 a.m. drunk after a night ''with the boys.'' Come to think of it, they argued a lot about who was at fault for Michael's shortcomings.

But right after Grace's senior year of high school,

things had changed. The long, hot summer had stretched by with Michael away looking at colleges. Grace had stayed behind, dutifully spending time with Jenna and being available for Michael's occasional long-distance calls.

Then one evening Jenna, who pronounced herself sick and tired of Grace's inactivity, talked her into going to the boardwalk over in Ocean City. Jenna met a guy in a T-shirt shop and disappeared with him, cropping up every half hour or so to promise Grace she'd just be "a few more minutes."

Grace had waited for an hour and a half, sitting there in her prissy sundress, wondering how Jenna got the nerve to just go off with some guy she didn't even know and do God-knows-what. Just as Grace was getting ready to give up and call a cab to take her home, Luke had shown up, like some dark knight in a white El Camino. He'd offered her a ride and, telling herself it beat paying for a 40-mile cab ride, she'd accepted.

But that wasn't entirely true. The prospect of riding all the way home with Luke wasn't exactly unappealing. In fact, it was sort of…exciting. Thrilling. Maybe even dangerous. Under the boardwalk lights, his dark hair gleaming and his skin tanned to brown, making his pale eyes seem even lighter, Luke certainly looked dangerous. That, contrasted with the unexpected chivalry of his offering to drive her home, had made him irresistible to her that night.

She watched him in the dim dash light as he drove home. His hands strong and capable on the wheel, forearms lean with sinewy muscle, his profile straight and masculine…by the time they made it back to Blue Moon Bay, Grace had kissed him a thousand times in her mind.

Although she could never know the evolution of his thoughts that night, he must have begun to see her in a new light too, because he didn't go directly to her house when they got to town. And she didn't ask him to. Instead, they circled the quiet streets by the shore, eventually stopping at the small Jolly George "Fun Park" at the end of the boardwalk, where there were a few ancient rides—a wooden roller coaster and a Ferris wheel, that were open in the summer evenings.

They walked through the park, neither touching nor drawing apart, for what seemed like hours, talking about everything. Grace wondered how she'd never seen this side of Luke before. Granted, he only showed the world his silent, somewhat intimidating, exterior. But she'd never even *imagined* the sensitivity he had; the fact that he was artistic and liked to draw; the fact that he worried about, and had taken care of, his father since his mother's death. It was hard to believe, but the guy who had been a thorn in her side since she'd begun dating his best friend was suddenly touching her heart as no one ever had before.

They were by the Ferris wheel when the guy who was running it announced that there would be just one more ride that evening. Grace, to whom Luke had just confided that he'd never gone on the rides here as a child, insisted that he had to go on with her. She wouldn't take no for an answer.

The Ferris wheel had only taken about five turns when it got stuck, with Grace and Luke at the top. It was the first time she realized she had a fear of heights. It was also the first time she realized that kisses could be more than a bland precursor to pleas for sex and guilt for not complying.

Grace lay on her bed now, aware of Jimmy down

the hall but caught up in the honeyed memory of a summer night that she'd stored away in the back of her mind for so long.

She closed her eyes and felt herself back in the cool metal seat next to Luke. It felt as if they were in space, a million miles from the bright lights and popcorn-strewn ground below. It was terrifying. When the wind lifted, the old seat squeaked on its hinges.

"What's wrong?" Luke had asked, just as she felt the blood drain from her face.

"We're stuck." It was stupid. She'd never been afraid of a Ferris wheel before.

Luke must have thought it was stupid too. "So what? He'll get it going again."

"Did you see that guy?" Grace's panic mounted. "Did you *smell* him? I bet that was a bottle of Mad Dog he had in his pocket."

Luke shrugged. "Either that or he was glad to see you."

"Luke, I'm serious." Her voice rose thinly. "I'm scared."

"Really?"

"Yes!"

"Shh. It's okay." He put an arm around her, a little awkwardly.

"How do you know? This thing's fifty years old if it's a day. It has to die sometime. Maybe this is the night."

"Nah." He was totally calm. "This happens all the time. These old motors overheat and just give out tem-porarily. Sparky down there will keep fidgeting with it, pushing the arm on and off, until it cools off some and starts to run again and he'll think he fixed it."

Grace laughed, despite her fear. Down below she

could see the ride operator doing just that. It made her feel better. "You're sure?"

"I guarantee it."

"Okay." She breathed. Her shoulders relaxed under his arm but he didn't move it. He probably just forgot, but she was glad. "In the meantime, we're trapped together," she said, testing for his response.

He looked into her eyes, making her shiver. "Yeah."

A moment passed.

"How long do you think it will be?"

"I don't know. Ten, maybe twenty, minutes."

"Ugh." She glanced back down at the flummoxed ride operator and felt woozy.

"Look up," Luke said quietly, lifting her chin with his index finger, then pointing to the stars. "You'll feel better."

He was right. The sky was a deep satin purple, so starry it seemed flecked like a dark tablecloth with spilled salt. She caught her breath. "It's beautiful."

"It is," he agreed, but he was looking at her, not the sky.

A thrill fluttered over her as she pretended not to notice. "It looks like the sky in a children's picture book."

"I don't know where you come up with this stuff," he said, shaking his head. "Everything's poetic to you."

"What's wrong with that?"

"Nothing." He smiled. "But what are you gonna do when you're out of school and you need to live in the real world?"

"I *do* live in the real world."

He gave a completely cynical shrug. "I wish." Then

he looked at her. "For what it's worth, though, I like it."

Did he like *her?* Before tonight, she wouldn't have thought so. "Maybe I should write children's books for a living, huh? Avoid the real world entirely."

He laughed. "Girls like you don't need to live in the real world. You'll marry someone rich and do whatever you want."

For some reason his saying that gave her a small pang. Not that she wanted to be with him or anything, but there was something disconcerting about him pawning her off on some imagined rich guy in her future. "So what happens to guys like you?"

He looked very serious. "I don't know."

She wanted to reach out to him. "What do you want?"

His gaze remained steady. "Doesn't matter."

She swallowed hard, trying to will away the desire that was snaking through her chest. Instead, she looked back over the edge of the seat. "So. This doesn't bother you a bit, huh?" She tried to laugh.

"I think you could say I'm bothered," Luke said softly, his gaze flickering from her face to her hair and back to her eyes, making her tingle as if he'd touched her.

"By the height?" she asked, looking up again so he wouldn't see the real question in her eyes.

"No."

Another moment passed, but something pulsed between them.

She turned to face him. "Then what?"

His mouth quirked up just a tiny bit on one side. "Now what do you think?"

"I don't know," she lied. She was terrified to say

anything else. Terrified that she was wrong, that he wasn't feeling what she was.

He stared into her eyes for a moment, then shook his head, laughing softly. "You do."

Electricity worked its way from the pit of her stomach to the center of her being. She shifted in her seat. "I don't know what you're talking about," she said haughtily, looking back at the sky.

"Don't you, Grace?"

"No, I don't." Her lips felt full with the desire to be kissed. It was crazy—he hadn't touched her, but she was experiencing every physical response in the book.

He didn't say a word.

Instead, she felt his hand on her face, turning it toward him, then he captured her mouth with his, in a kiss so deep that it left her gasping.

"Now *that* makes me nervous," he said huskily, his hand still cupping her cheek.

For a moment, she stared at him wordlessly, trembling in the warm night air. Then, following an impulse she'd never even dreamed of, she initiated another kiss.

He responded hungrily, opening his mouth under her parted lips and drinking her in so thoroughly that he might have taken some of her soul.

He moved his strong hands down her ribcage, across the thin cotton of her sundress. She felt safe in his grasp. Warm. Excited. He drove her wild yet at the same time made her feel utterly secure.

She raised her hands, twining her fingers in his thick dark hair, and pulled his mouth still closer, if that was possible. She wanted to stop him from stopping. As her mouth moved against his, she pressed herself against him, begging wordlessly for him to continue, to keep kissing her forever.

It felt as though he would. They groped at each other like the teenagers they were, touching, tasting, fumbling. Their teeth knocked together and they smiled, but only for a moment, before the fever of lust took them over again and they took it deeper, tongues touching, exploring, lingering.

"I hope we stay stuck here all night," Grace breathed.

"It'll cool off." He spanned her lower back with his hands, then slowly moved her legs across his lap.

"I hope not," she managed to say before drowning in sensation.

Luke's hand moved across her hip, then her thigh, caressing her in broad, languid movements.

She relaxed her legs, parting them slightly.

He edged his hand higher and higher on her thigh, raising her dress with it, then slipped his hand between her legs, pressing gently against her. Only the thinnest fabric lay between his skin and hers.

Grace tried to catch her breath but couldn't, arching against him, begging silently for more. She felt him smile against her mouth for a moment, then he complied, artfully touching her as if she were naked.

She might as well have been for the dizzying response she had. She reached for the front of his jeans and felt his hardness behind the thick denim and stiff zipper. With shaking hands, she fumbled with his belt buckle, but froze when he slipped a finger around the cotton crotch of her underwear and plunged a finger into her.

She'd never felt like this before. Never let Michael this close. She didn't know what insanity was making her allow Luke to do it, but it was too late, she couldn't stop.

She didn't want to stop.

His instincts were perfect. He weakened her with every stroke, instinctively knowing when to tease her and when to enter her. Her heart pounded so hard she thought it would burst, but she didn't care. All that mattered was this moment, this man, this feeling.

And then, in a moment, something exploded inside of her, leaving her clinging to him and shuddering, as wave after wave of pleasure splashed upon the shore of her resolve.

It seemed to go on forever, then slowly the world came back into focus, with just a few shimmering streamers of ecstasy drifting through the sky before her.

"I—" She couldn't speak. "I've never—"

He silenced her with a gentle kiss.

She held herself against his shoulder, burying her face in the crook of his neck.

The wind rose, and the seat creaked again. It had probably been creaking the whole time, only she hadn't noticed.

"I've never done that before," she said finally, in a rush of breath.

Luke touched her cheek tenderly.

"We shouldn't have...this is crazy..."

He pulled back and looked at her with sharp eyes. "What?"

"Well, I mean, Michael..."

For a moment, he looked as if she'd slapped him. "Right. Michael."

Something in her deflated.

"He's probably been calling, wondering where I am," she said, trying to think what she'd say to Michael about tonight.

Luke let out a long breath. "We'd better tell him the truth about this."

"No!" She could imagine his response. He'd be *livid.* "No, we can't."

"It'll be okay," Luke said. "You want me to talk to him?"

"Oh, God, no, you can't. Let me think." But her mind was blank. Luke had erased everything. It wasn't that she wanted to maintain her relationship with Michael. After what had just happened, she couldn't imagine going back to him. She just didn't want to end it in an explosion of jealousy and accusation. "If it looks like I ran off with his best friend, it will humiliate him."

"Look, I'll just tell him I made a pass at you," Luke said, before she had the chance to tell him what she was thinking. His voice had cooled. "But that nothing really happened. That's the truth, after all. Nothing much *really* happened. It's not like we did it all."

Nothing had happened? She had been intimate with him in a way she'd never been intimate with anyone, in a way she'd intended to save for her wedding night, but Luke thought *nothing* had happened?

Shame burned in her cheeks. "That's right. Nothing happened. So why get Michael involved? He'll just be mad at both of us, and for no real reason."

The Ferris wheel jerked to life, easily lowering them to the ground.

"Perfect timing," Luke noted. "I guess it's a sign. Come on, I'll take you home."

In the end, neither one of them had to tell Michael. Susan Howard, who lived across the street from Grace and who had a massive crush on Michael, told him she'd seen Luke drop Grace off *very* late one night. It was all he needed to hear. He'd immediately jumped to the wrong—or maybe really the right—conclusion.

It had ended his friendship with Luke and nearly ended his relationship with Grace. She'd jumped through hoops to preserve it. As much as it embarrassed her to recall it now, she had apologized profusely and promised never to talk to Luke again. And she hadn't.

Not until the day she'd walked into his office asking for a job.

Chapter Six

It was still muggy outside at 7:00 p.m. A milky haze of mist hung over the soccer field, with a great orange ball of sun dipping lower behind the goalposts. The buzz of locusts filled the evening air.

Luke waited for her by the barn. He was grinding out the stub of a cigarette with his toe when she walked up.

"Thought you stopped that years ago," she said to him.

"Did," he said, with a puff of smoke. "Just every once in a while…"

She shrugged, thinking of the entire box of chocolate marshmallow cookies she'd consumed during a marathon viewing of *Pride and Prejudice* after Michael had left. She was hardly one to point fingers. "I guess we all do things that aren't good for us once in a while."

He looked at her for a moment. "Yeah, well, I won't tell if you won't."

She hesitated. Was he talking about smoking or...? Or nothing. Of course he meant smoking. "I'm not going to tell," she said flippantly. "The kids don't need to know what a dubious role model you really are."

He raised an eyebrow, resting his gaze on hers for a moment. "Think you're a better one?"

She straightened. "I'll be an excellent influence, Luke. You know I was a great student. You used to make fun of me for it all the time."

He gave a laugh and started off toward the bus, like the Pied Piper, so sure she would follow him that he didn't even look back.

She did.

"I don't think I made fun of you for being a good student," he said lazily. "As I recall, it was for sucking up to the teachers."

"I did *not* suck up to the teachers!"

"Geez, Grace, you needed an extra locker just for all the polished red apples you brought in for Mrs. MacGonagle."

"Once," Grace said, her face going hot immediately. She had taken so much grief for that. "*Once* I brought in apples for Mrs. MacGonagle, and it was only because my mother told her we had such a huge harvest from the apple tree that she was going to have to throw them away if no one wanted them. And they *weren't* polished."

"Okay," Luke said, splaying his arms as he walked. "If you say so."

"What about you? As I recall you were an all-A

student, even while you were doing your broody James Dean thing. You even got that big scholarship.''

''I never sucked up.'' He smiled, but it was a smile that said he didn't want to talk about anything personal if it had to do with himself. He kept walking until he got to the bus. ''Okay,'' he said, leaning on the yellow vehicle. ''Go to it.''

''Okay.'' If he didn't want to talk about it, they wouldn't talk about it.

She walked past him and into the bus. He followed this time.

It was as hot as a sauna inside. ''Comfortable?'' Grace asked with a wan smile. ''If not, I can turn on the air conditioner. Oh, wait, there *isn't* an air conditioner.''

''I'm fine,'' Luke said. ''But if you're hot, go ahead and turn on the fan. That should help.''

She gave him a look. ''You've never driven this bus in the summer, have you?''

''Sure I have. Now get going so you can pass the test and drive it yourself this summer.''

''All right, all right.'' She proceeded to complete the safety check she'd have to perform for the final portion of the test on Friday. She checked the windows, the locks, the lights and signals, gauges, seat belts, mats, steering wheel and everything else that moved, lit, opened, closed, signaled or stuck out.

Including the Bodily Fluid Clean-up Kit.

''Which looks fine,'' Grace pronounced, sitting in the driver's seat backward, facing Luke. ''Now. Did I forget anything?''

He shook his head. ''Just remember to take the keys out of the ignition when you're finished. Carol Borden forgot that twice.''

Was he ever, even once, going to admit she'd done a good job? She doubted it. To Luke, it seemed, complimenting Grace would mean a huge compromise of his principles. If she drove the bus through a flood and around a tornado, saving scores of children in her charge, he'd probably only comment on whether or not she fully depressed the parking brake afterward.

She leaned back against the steering wheel and crossed her arms in front of her. "So why do you know all this, Luke? Is it a prerequisite for becoming the headmaster?"

"I was the driver here for five years."

"Right," she scoffed, picking idly at some duct tape that was covering a hole on the back of the seat. "After that football scholarship to Stanford, you decided to come back home and drive a bus."

"I didn't go to Stanford," he said quietly.

Grace was about to toss off a joke when she noticed how still his expression was and realized he wasn't kidding. "You're serious! You didn't go at all?"

"Nope."

Suddenly the buzz of the locusts outside seemed very loud.

"Why not?" she asked. "I thought it was a done deal."

He shrugged. "Nothing's ever really a done deal, I guess. Good lesson to learn early."

The scholarship, she remembered well, had been very important to Luke. It was an incredible accomplishment. His parents hadn't had much money to begin with, but when his mother had died—when he was, what, in ninth grade? Grace wasn't sure—they'd lost half their income. Luke had taken a part-time job at the Texaco station, but his college prospects looked bleak until his spectacular senior year, when the scouts had come to check him out. His scholarship had been a *huge* deal in Blue Moon Bay. Even the newspaper covered it.

"Why on earth didn't you go, Luke?" Grace asked, increasingly curious. Had he just blown it off? Too cool for school? "It was such a great opportunity."

"It just didn't work out," he said shortly. "Bad timing. Forget it, it doesn't matter now."

"Well, sure it matters—"

"No." His tone was hard, and left no room for argument. "It doesn't."

Grace looked at him wordlessly for a moment. What had happened to him? How had she never heard anything about it? Maybe she'd just been gone for too long. She was out of the Blue Moon Bay loop.

"What time are you scheduled to take the driving test on Friday?" Luke asked, taking a folded paper out of his back pocket.

It was clear he wasn't going to talk about it anymore. She'd have to get the scoop from someone else. "Three," she answered, trying to sound as if she wasn't still stuck on the scholarship thing.

"All right. Chuck Borden's going to drive up with you, since you're not allowed to drive the bus without a commercially licensed driver until you have a CDL yourself."

"Is Chuck the Spanish teacher?"

"He is. But he's also the other bus driver. He took the run in order to earn a little extra. It works well for him, but it also means that he's on a tight schedule. He does his run, then starts his classes. He won't be available as back-up for you."

"Who says I'm going to need back-up?"

"No one. I hope."

"Well, I won't," she said with determination. "I'll be here every day."

"Assuming you pass the test. Don't get ahead of yourself, or you'll lose sight of that goal."

"I don't think so. I'm very well aware that the test is coming up."

"You worried?"

"No," she lied. "Not a bit."

His mouth quirked into a half-smile as he leaned forward and handed her the piece of paper he'd taken out of his pocket. "This is the route you're going to be taking Monday morning. Assuming you pass the test."

"I'll pass," she said, studying the list. Some of the students were quite far-flung. "This is going to take forever."

"It's about an hour."

"You really do need transportation," she mused. "This one here on Saltside Lane would take half an hour to get to if you took a direct route. It would be hard for nine-to-fivers to get a kid here and still get to work on time unless one of the parents were working in town. And, God knows, there aren't any jobs here."

Luke gave a half smile, then said, "That's Donald Henderson. He's one of our scholarship kids. There's no way in the world his parents could get him here themselves."

She looked at the remaining addresses, and the geography of Blue Moon Bay and the surrounding area came back to her with complete clarity. Some of the students lived in multimillion-dollar homes in Cape Trayhorn Estates, and some lived in rowhouses along the main streets of town.

"You know, I never thought I'd be driving my own kid around Blue Moon Bay to school, much less anyone else's." She sighed. "So much for moving up in life."

"What the hell's wrong with you, Grace?" Luke asked in a sharp voice.

She was startled by his question and his tone. "What do you mean?"

"Why have you always been so down on Blue Moon Bay? Ever since I've known you, you've talked about getting out of here, like it's some kind of hellhole. It's a nice town, Grace, and it's home to a lot of nice people."

Humiliation filled her. "I didn't mean to insult anyone, Luke, it's just not the place I want to be."

"You say that like anyone who *does* want to be here is some stupid peasant who doesn't know any better." He stood up and started for the door, then stopped and looked her dead in the eye. "As long as I've known you, you've wanted things bigger, better." He hesitated, then added, "Richer. How's it working out for you?"

She gaped at him in silence, completely unable to formulate a response.

"Good luck on the test," he said abruptly, then left, shaking his head.

She watched him for a moment, then sprang from the seat and out into the thick evening air behind him. "Wait a minute, Luke!"

He stopped, and she could see him take a long breath before turning to face her. As though he was mustering patience.

That galled her.

"What?" he asked wearily.

"You don't know what you're talking about." She wished she had a better argument, but the words had been stunned right out of her. They'd come back tonight, probably, around midnight. "You don't know me at all," she said lamely.

"You're right—I don't. I only know what I see."

She went to him boldly and stood before him. "What do you see, Luke? Huh? What do you see?"

He looked down at her, and for a moment she saw tenderness cross his expression. But it was only for a moment, and it was gone quickly. "It doesn't matter what I see."

"No," she said, wishing she really felt that way. "That's right, it doesn't matter. So keep it to yourself, okay?"

"You're absolutely right, that's what I should have done in the first place."

"You bet it is. You know, you don't have a clue what I've been through." Self-pity rose in her breast, but she pushed it back down. It was enough that she knew she was a good person and, more than that, a good mother. She was proud of the way she'd held it together when Michael left, proud that Jimmy thought of her as strong and brave and someone who could take care of him when he was sad and confused. She hadn't let him see her tears, or her anger, and she was proud of herself for that too.

Whatever it was that Luke hated so much about her was going to have to be his own problem. She couldn't afford to let it affect her own confidence and self-esteem. She'd already taken enough of a beating in that regard.

"And you can just go to hell, Luke Stewart," she fumed, stalking past him to her car.

He said something behind her, but she didn't hear what it was and she didn't want to stop and ask. She just kept going until she got to the old BMW that had seemed like such a prize once, and got in, praying it would start.

It did, thank God, and she whipped out of the driveway without looking back at him.

He was glad she hadn't heard his apology. He didn't want to apologize, damn it, it had been burning in him for so long.

Ever since that night on the Ferris wheel a thousand years ago.

He'd wanted her for a long time before that night, though it wasn't something he went around talking about. For one thing, it was a betrayal of Michael, though he richly deserved it, but for another, Luke just wasn't the kind of guy who needed anyone or anything. It was embarrassing to spend as much time as he did pining for a girl, much less one he could never have.

Then there had been that one brief moment, the unbelievable luck of finding her in Ocean City, when it had seemed as if maybe—just maybe—he wasn't crazy to think he might have a shot with her. That maybe she felt the same way he did.

It was over quickly, though. Of course. Just as he was about to brave the subject, she'd raised the specter of Michael, making it very clear that she didn't want him to know. She was terrified of losing Michael, it seemed, and not because she loved him. Hell, if she'd loved him, she wouldn't have been with Luke. No, she wanted the Bowes name and everything that went with it. She wanted to be half of the golden couple of Blue Moon Bay. No matter what the cost.

For a while, Luke hadn't wanted to believe that Grace was so shallow. But Michael had told him exactly what the arrangement was, just a few months after they'd gotten married. While Grace had stayed behind, pregnant, Michael had come back to town for his grandmother's funeral. During that short week, Michael had slept with at least two women that Luke knew of. Just like in high school. As a matter of fact, he'd left Harley's Bar with one of them about ten minutes after bragging to Luke about the "open arrangement" he and Grace had in their marriage.

She made the deal with me. She's got what she wants, Michael had told Luke. *Big house, imported car, President of the Junior League. And I get a good-looking arm piece when I have to go out.*

So what do you want with someone like Mary Jo Wiley? Luke had asked, indicating one of the tight-jeaned women who was waving to Michael from the bar.

Excitement, man. Michael's laugh had been harsh. *Heat. Grace is as cold as ice in the bedroom.*

Luke knew with some certainty that *that* wasn't true. Or if it was, it wasn't her fault.

Still, who was he to question what went on in someone else's marriage? It was their problem, not his.

His problem, now, was that Michael was history, and Grace was back, and some part of Luke's eighteen-year-old libido remembered her.

Jimmy held tightly onto his mother's hand. He knew it was babyish, but he was just so excited he couldn't help it.

For the first time, he was beginning to feel like maybe this town wasn't so bad. Maybe he actually even liked the quiet streets and the big yards and the fact that he was able to get a dog—a real, live *dog*—for the first time in his life.

They were at the pound, although his mother called it the humane society, and a guy in a blue uniform was opening a door for them to go look at the dogs.

As soon as he stepped through, Jimmy smiled. He couldn't help it. The room smelled like pee and the sound of yelping and barking was so loud, he could barely hear his mom telling him to keep his fingers out of the cage, but to him it was heaven.

He walked slowly up the cement aisle, being sure to make eye contact with each dog along the way. He was positive that when he saw *his* dog, he'd know it. He walked past big scruffy dogs, and little happy dogs, and sleek dogs, and sleeping dogs, but only one dog came over and poked his nose through the metal fence at Jimmy. After that, he didn't *need* to look in the dog's hopeful brown eyes to know.

"This is the one," he announced.

His mother frowned and came over to him. "Really?" She poked a finger through the cage—just what she'd told Jimmy not to do—and the dog licked her excitedly. "Are you sure?"

"I'm sure. And his name is…" He thought for a minute. Last night when he was lying in bed, the name he'd come up with had seemed so perfect. Now, though, he was afraid it was a little dumb.

"What's his name?" his mom asked.

He decided to go ahead and say it. After all, his mom never laughed at him, but she'd tell him the truth. "It's Tonto. Do you think that's too goofy?"

"No, it's great. Look, he even answers to it. Tonto!" She made her voice high. "Tonto! Here, boy!"

The little dog looked up and tilted his head to the side, wagging his tail.

"See?" She laughed. "That's his name, all right."

Jimmy smiled and touched the dog's cold nose. "What kind of breed do you think he is?"

"He looks a little like a Jack Russell terrier. With, maybe, some springer spaniel or something mixed in. I'm not sure." She stood up and smoothed her skirt down. She was all dressed up to go to some big test in the afternoon. "Are you sure this is the one you want, Jimmy?" she asked seriously. "Because you can't just bring him back, you know."

"I know. This is the one I want. And I'll *never* want to give him back," he said ferociously, thinking of his father and how long it had been since he'd come to see Jimmy and his mom. *"Ever."*

Later that night, Grace had her own taste of excitement.

"Congratulations, you're a bus driver!" Jenna raised her champagne glass and clinked it against Grace's, sloshing the fizzy drink onto their hands.

"Thank you, thank you very much." Grace raised her glass to her lips and closed her eyes, relishing the yeasty taste of her favorite vintage. She had half a case of it left—one of the more valuable parts of her divorce settlement—and the way things were going, she might just work her way through it this weekend.

She raised her glass to her new license, which she and Jenna had propped against a candle in the middle of the table. "To me," she said with a giggle. "Oh, and to Bob for taking care of all the kids—and the dog—tonight, so we could have a girls' night."

"To Bob," Jenna repeated, raising her own glass

again. She took a sip then set it down and asked, "Say, where's your mom?"

"Bridge club."

Jenna frowned. "I thought they met during the day."

"She's got a bunch of them now." Grace shrugged. "Several of them meet at night. In fact, they go really late." Silently, Grace hoped that she didn't end up at the high end of middle-aged alone and filling her time with card-playing.

"Ooh, maybe she'll meet someone." Jenna smiled. "Some dashing, card-playing Omar Sharif type."

"Please," Grace said. "Mother hasn't been on a date since before I was born. I can't even imagine her starting now."

Jenna nodded. "It would be weird. But what about you? Think you're going to get back into dating here?"

Grace groaned. "Who would I go out with? You snagged the only good man in Blue Moon Bay. And he's not even *from* here." Bob had moved into town ten years ago when he'd got a job with a carpentry company. He and Jenna had met when she'd hired him to build bookshelves.

Jenna raised an eyebrow. "I can think of one or two guys here who used to be interesting to you," she said in a sing-songy voice.

"My track record with old Blue Moon love interests isn't so good, Jen."

"Well, Michael didn't turn out so hot, but maybe someone else would. Let's do your tarot cards and see," Jenna said eagerly, reaching for her bag. "I brought them along so I could practice on you."

"No, no, no, I don't believe in those things."

"So what's the harm then?" Jenna asked, opening

a small leather pouch. "Just do it for fun. Here." She thrust the large deck into Grace's hands. "Shuffle."

"This is stupid," Grace protested, shuffling.

"No, it's not. Now cut the deck."

"I don't believe any of it." She cut the deck.

"The cards will tell," Jenna said, in a spooky voice, then laughed. "Pick one and put it here, then put the next one here."

Grace picked cards according to Jenna's direction, and Jenna set them up in an elaborate layout. Finally, with ten cards facedown on the table in the shape of a pentagon, she put the rest of the deck aside and started turning the cards over.

"This is where you are right now," Jenna said. "This card represents whatever is either helping or hindering you. Hmm. The king of cups." She considered the card. "A man with dark hair and blue eyes. Who could that be?"

"This is rigged." Grace grabbed the book from Jenna and read the description for herself. Sure enough, it said the card could indicate a man with dark hair and blue eyes. A powerful yet fair man. An honest man.

Or it could represent those qualities, perhaps in someone else Grace knew. That's what it had to mean, she figured, not an actual man with dark hair and blue eyes. And certainly not Luke Stewart, who, when last she'd seen him, had lambasted her for no good reason. She looked closer. The book didn't say anything about personal attacks.

"*You* picked the card," Jenna reminded her lightly, taking back the book. "This guy looks pretty significant in your life. Maybe a boss?" She winked. "In any event, you should be hearing from him soon."

"Like on Monday? When I go to work? Remarkable prediction."

Jenna ignored her sarcasm. "And there's something about a journey. Maybe that's driving the bus."

Grace thought of the long route Luke had drawn up for her. "It's going to feel like a journey. Every day." Privately, she thought about her return to Blue Moon Bay and what a journey that had been, both literally and figuratively. What about the future journey back to New Jersey? Was she really going to be able to do that in a year, as she'd planned? Already, she was in a bigger financial hole than she'd anticipated. Grace had a bad feeling that her budget wasn't going to work out quite the way she'd hoped.

"Well, don't worry, there's great prosperity here too. A *huge* fortune or inheritance." She looked up at Grace. "Got any fabulously rich relatives I don't know about?"

Grace flashed her a wry grin. "If I do, I don't know about them either."

Jenna looked back at the cards, then at the book she was using to check her interpretations. "Maybe it's going to be more of a *spiritual* fortune. Yup, three of cups, here's another love card."

Grace watched, sipping her champagne with increasing frequency, as Jenna told her that her entire future was wrapped up with this dark-haired, blue-eyed man.

What if that were true? Grace wondered. Could she even imagine getting involved with a new man? It wasn't that she still felt stung by Michael. Enough time had passed that she'd grown to realize she and Michael had *never* had the kind of close relationship she'd pretended they did. He didn't get her jokes. Didn't care about her life or her interests. Barely even showed any curiosity about their son. She was better off without him, and she knew that now.

But a new man? It was hard to picture. When she tried to imagine someone like the man Jenna described, all she could see was Luke Stewart.

And he *certainly* wasn't a romantic interest for her. Or vice versa. That couldn't be more plain.

When she was finished with the reading, Jenna sat back and said, "The cards don't lie."

Grace brought her focus back to Jenna. "Maybe not, but I'm not so sure about the reader."

"Hey, I object to that! Out of seventy-six cards, you picked these ten. Check the interpretations yourself." Jenna thumped her hand on the *Mother Earth Tarot* book on the table. "It's very clear."

Grace rolled her eyes. "Then I guess a tall, dark stranger will be coming to town to sweep me off my feet soon." She shook her head. "Seriously, Jenna, that'd be great for starry-eyed teenagers who want their fortunes told, because you know there's *always* romance in their future, but I'm not buying this for me *at all*."

"Suit yourself." Jenna gathered the cards and put them back in the case. "I'm not sure how much I believe myself, but you have to admit, it *is* interesting that all the cards you picked were so consistent about this guy."

"And so wrong," Grace added.

"Maybe." Jenna poured more champagne into both their glasses. "I've got an idea! Let's call him!"

"Who?"

"Luke! Just like we used to in high school!" She dissolved into a fit of giggles. "Remember when we called Kenny Harrison and had him convinced that we were aliens who were coming to get him at midnight?''

Grace couldn't help laughing with her. Although Jenna had been the one doing the calling and the talking, Grace had listened with fascination on the other line as Kenny had asked what to pack.

"Come on, let's call Luke," Jenna persisted, taking the cordless phone from the table and pushing the Talk button.

Grace wrestled the receiver from her grasp. "No way. We're not teenagers anymore. We're mothers. Mature women. We don't pull that kind of prank." The dial tone blared between them. "Especially not with caller ID and Star-Sixty-Nine technologies out there. And *especially* not with Luke Stewart. Our relationship is bad enough."

Jenna took her hand off the phone. "You just had a little spat. You guys *always* had spats, and, as you know, there was a definite attraction."

It was hard to deny, at least to Jenna, who had always known the truth. "Yeah, well, we're not always attracted to the people who are best for us, are we?"

"No, that's true," Jenna agreed. "But sometimes you just don't know until you give someone a chance. Even someone like Luke."

"Even if I were willing, and I'm *not,* Luke doesn't have any interest in me. He hates me."

"I don't think so. And I know you don't hate him." She wasn't going to give up. "Let's go to his house. Look in the windows and see if he has a girlfriend."

Grace tossed the phone onto the sofa several yards away. "I couldn't care less if he has a girlfriend or not." She tried to sound nonchalant, but she *did* kind of wonder about his private life.

"Come on, admit you're curious. Let's go."

Grace shook her head. "On top of the fact that it's *illegal* to spy on people through their windows, we've been drinking. We can't drive."

"We'll walk."

"We're not *interested*." Grace hesitated. "Although there is one thing I'm interested in. Do you have any idea why Luke didn't go off to college at Stanford, like he was supposed to?"

Jenna looked blank. "I didn't even know he was supposed to."

"Yes, you did—he got a scholarship, remember? It was a huge deal."

"Hmm. That *sort of* rings a bell. But I don't know. Why?"

Grace shrugged. "He mentioned the other day that he hadn't gone but he wouldn't say why. The whole thing just seems strange to me."

"So you *do* care about him."

Grace felt her face grow warm. "I'm just curious. Aren't you?"

"Not particularly. But if you really want to know what happened, we could ask the cards."

Grace snorted. "Oh, come on, the cards don't know squat."

"I don't know, Grace, it seems to me they were uncannily correct for you."

"About what? About a man in my life? There isn't one. A journey? Not going anywhere. And a great fortune? *Please*. If I had that, I wouldn't be driving a bus."

"You have to be a little patient," said Jenna, unflappable. "This is the *future* we're looking at. The cards clearly said—"

Fortunately, Jenna was interrupted by the ringing of the doorbell, although Grace had the uneasy feeling that she was going to be hearing a lot about what "the cards said" in the future.

"I was in the neighborhood," Luke said when she opened the door. "I tried to call, but the line was busy. I hope you don't mind me dropping by."

Chapter Seven

The champagne hit her full-force as soon as she saw him.

"Uh. N-no," Grace stammered. "I'm just surprised."

"Look, about the other day. I shouldn't have said that stuff. It wasn't my place." It wasn't quite an apology, but she thought it was as close as she was going to get to one.

"Forget it." She tried to gather her wits as they scattered like cockroaches in the light. "Do you want to come in? Have a drink?" She stepped back and gestured into the house.

He didn't move, though his eyes flicked briefly behind her. "No, thanks. Did you pass the test?"

She smiled. "Yes, I did."

"Good."

"What, did you expect me to fail?" she demanded happily.

He gave a short laugh. "Since the day you walked into the garage at school, I haven't known what to expect."

Grace felt light-headed and silently cursed the champagne.

It was making her giddy. "Is that all bad?"

The porch light gleamed off his glossy hair. He looked like a model or something. A shampoo ad.

"Why are you looking at me that way?"

"What way?" She pulled herself together. "I wasn't looking at you any way in particular. I just…I thought I saw a spider."

"Ah." He nodded as if he were talking to a crazy person.

"It's gone now."

"Oh, my God, *Luke Stewart?*" Jenna gasped from behind Grace. "I can't believe it, we were *just* talking about you."

"No, we weren't," Grace said quickly.

"Yes, we—"

"No, that was something else," Grace said. Then, with a pointed look at Jenna, Grace stepped out onto the front porch with Luke, closing the door behind her before Jenna could say anything more. "Don't want to let the bugs in," she explained with a fast smile.

"You were talking about me?"

How did he do that, that almost-smile of his? How did he manage to look amused and above-it-all at the same time?

He was *cool,* that was how. He'd always been cool, even though he'd been an ace student, which was normally *not* considered cool at Bayside High School. But

Luke gave off an aura of not needing anyone or anything.

Girls found it irresistible.

Not Grace, though. She had no trouble resisting him. "We weren't talking about you," she said. "We were talking about my job. Celebrating it, actually. We had a little champagne." She was babbling and forced herself to stop.

The hum of the locusts rose around them, harmonizing with the chirping crickets.

"Well, I'm glad you passed," he said, in a tone that suggested he was wrapping things up.

She didn't want him to leave. Not yet. She wanted, somehow, to make things feel normal between them, so there weren't awkward silences. "Have a seat," she said, a little too eagerly, indicating the porch swing.

He watched as she went over and sat there herself. She stopped short of patting the spot next to her.

"I don't want to interrupt your celebration," he said, standing still under the light. "I just came by to see about the test and to give you these." He reached into the front pocket of his jeans, took out a small key ring with two keys on it and tossed them to her.

Remarkably, she caught them, and closed her hand around them as if they were alive. They were warm from his body heat. "What are these for?"

"The bus," he said, cocking his head slightly and giving her half a smile. An I-know-you're-tipsy-so-I'll-be-patient half smile. "Remember?"

"Well, yes." She felt her face grow hot. Of *course* they were the bus keys, what was she *thinking?* Two small glasses, that was all she'd had. "I just meant..." She felt the keys, searching for an excuse for her stupid coy act. "There are two of them. What's the second one to?"

"It's a spare. Keep it in your wallet or something, in case you lock yourself out."

"I'm not going to lock myself out."

"Okay. Just in case."

"Geez, you have no faith in me at all."

"Don't take it personally, Grace. I don't have faith in anyone."

She suspected he was kidding, but she couldn't stop herself from baiting him. "*Especially* me, Luke. You've *never* had faith in me."

He gave a broad shrug. "I have as much faith in you as I need to. I'm sure you'll do a fine job."

Fine. She'd always hated that word. "Thanks," she said half-heartedly.

"Grace? Are you pouting?" He definitely looked amused.

"No."

"Good."

"Fine."

Quiet settled between them.

"So, I guess I'll go," Luke said, starting to turn.

"Wait, Luke." She felt as though she had to stop him. As though she had somehow to *fix* their conversation before she let him go. Before it got stuck in his brain as one more Bad Experience with Grace.

He looked back. God, had his eyes always been so blue? "What?"

She scrambled for something to say but came up short. "Nothing. I just…making sure…school starts at nine?"

"Nine-fifteen."

"Ah. Well, there you go. Good thing I asked."

He gave her a curious look but said, "Right. Wouldn't want to get them there too early."

She nodded and tried to look as if she was taking in more than just the sight of him, standing there looking sexy in the thick, hot air. She fully realized it was the champagne that made him look so good, and she didn't want to say or do anything she'd regret later. "Good to know," she said.

"Grace?"

"Hmm?"

"I was kidding. It doesn't matter if they get there early. Just don't get them in late."

She forced herself to stop nodding and just leveled her eyes on his. "Deal."

"You've got the list of students that I gave you the other day?"

"In my car."

"You're sure you haven't lost them?"

"I haven't lost them, Luke, come on, what kind of idiot do you think you're dealing with?"

"Did I say you were an idiot?"

"Not in so many words, but you didn't expect me to pass the test and you don't expect me to be able to keep track of the key, and now you're at least half convinced that I've lost the list of students I'm supposed to pick up. Is it me, or have you had really big problems with bus drivers in the past?"

He hesitated, making her fear the worst and fear that he was going to say it out loud.

"This has been a difficult couple of months around the school," he said finally. "A lot of things that shouldn't have gone wrong, have. I'm just trying to keep as much as I can under control."

"Are you including me with those things you want to control?"

"I'm including the school transportation." He gave nothing away with his eyes. "Okay?"

"Okay."

He looked down, as if he were turning to leave, then added, "A man would have to be crazy to try and control you."

She gave a hollow laugh. "Have you been talking to Michael or something?"

"Not for a long time."

She knew that. She'd only been joking. But the way he answered made her think Luke knew something about her and Michael that perhaps she didn't. "How long?" she asked.

"How long ago did his grandmother die?"

She thought about it. "I was about seven months pregnant at the time, so that would be, what, eleven years? That was the last time you spoke with him?"

"That was it."

"And what did you talk about?"

He started to say something, then clearly changed his mind. "Who the hell remembers, Grace? Eleven years is a long time."

"I can remember things that happened longer ago than that, believe it or not," she said, remembering the Ferris wheel. It was incredible how that memory made her heart accelerate even now.

"You referring to something in particular?"

She gave a wan smile. "You hoping I am?"

He met her gaze evenly. "I remember a thing or two from the past myself."

"Do you think about it often? The past, I mean."

"Not when I can help it."

"Can you help it often?"

He studied her for a moment, then gave a slow nod. "As often as I can."

She couldn't win with him. She wanted to just say, *Come on, Luke, do you think about me? Do you ever lie in the dark at night and think about that night? Do you ever wonder what would have happened if either one of us had had the nerve to give us a try?* But she didn't say anything of the sort.

And he didn't give anything away.

"All right, then." He lingered for just a moment more, then said, "I'd better go on my way. I'll see you Monday. Good luck."

Grace wasn't usually a late sleeper, so it was a real surprise to her on Monday morning when she woke up almost an hour later than she'd planned. A quick check of her alarm clock showed that she'd set a.m. and p.m. backward, and it hadn't gone off at all.

Fortunately Jimmy was already up and dressed. He had also eaten three bowls of sugary cereal. It was better than nothing, though, Grace figured. She, on the other hand, had no time to eat, no time even to shower, no time to do anything except throw on some clothes and perch a baseball cap on her head.

The drive to Connor School should have taken ten minutes, but she got there in seven. By the time she unlocked the bus, it was just a few minutes later than she'd originally planned to leave.

Congratulating herself, she sat down in the driver's seat and produced the keys. "Ready, buddy?" she asked, looking at Jimmy in the rearview mirror. She was glad that he'd opted to ride with her instead of hanging out on the campus. He was good company and surprisingly good moral support.

"Are *you?*" he asked, smiling. To him, this was a thrill almost on par with an amusement-park ride.

She was glad to see it. He'd been glum about the prospect of summer school all week. "Of course I am. Boy, if your dad could see me now, huh?"

"I don't think he'd believe it."

Not only would he not believe it, she thought, he would *never* approve of it. In fact, Grace would go so far as to say that if Michael knew now that she was driving their son around in a school bus, he'd probably try to take some sort of legal action to stop it. She smiled at the thought and, with great relish, turned the key.

Nothing happened.

She tried again. Nothing. Just a click.

She muttered an oath.

"What's wrong?" Jimmy asked.

"I'm not sure," she said, looking at her watch. She should have been on Sycamore by now. "It's a no go." She resisted the urge to slam her fist against the steering wheel. "Okay, let's see here, what could be wrong?" She went through a mental list of the engine parts and what would happen if any of them malfunctioned.

"Maybe the battery's dead," Jimmy suggested.

"I think it would crank if the battery was dead," she said, remembering the time Michael had reamed her out for continuing to try to start the car when it wouldn't turn over. *You're going to ruin the ignition,* he'd said. *If it cranks like that but doesn't turn over, the battery needs a jump start. For God's sake, call triple-A.*

"I'm going to have to go tell someone," she decided as she said the words. Who could she tell apart from Luke? she wondered frantically. She still had a triple-A card, but she knew that probably went against some kind of protocol. Besides, she was clearly going to be late for all of her pick-ups—it wasn't as if she could just sit here in the bus waiting for help without telling anyone.

While Jimmy waited outside, Grace went in the main door of the school and explained the situation to the bubbly redheaded secretary, Judy Flynn.

Judy frowned as she listened, then said, "Wait right here while I go try and find someone to take a look at it."

That sounded hopeful, Grace thought. She sat down in one of the visitors' waiting chairs, in front of a brightly colored papier-mâchè sculpture that looked as if it had been done by a student. *Someone* might be someone other than Luke, Grace speculated. Maybe Judy would just go call the garage where they normally had their mechanical work done.

No such luck.

"What'd you do to the bus, Grace?" Luke asked as soon as Judy returned with him.

She wasn't sure, but she thought he looked slightly amused. "I didn't do anything to it," she said, standing up. "I got in and tried to start it, but it's dead. Nothing happens when I turn the key."

"Does it crank?"

She sighed. "I would have said it cranks if it cranked, Luke. *Nothing* happens."

"All right, let's take a look."

"Shouldn't we call a mechanic or something?"

"I hope not."

"But it's dead."

He looked at her. "Maybe it can be resurrected. If not, you can take Chuck's bus when he gets in." He stopped at the front desk. "Call the parents, Jude. Tell them we're running a little late."

"Okey-dokey," she chirped.

Jude, Grace noticed, with more irritation for that than for her *okey-dokey* response. They seemed awfully chummy. How old was she anyway? Nineteen? Twenty?

"Grace?" Luke said, startling her. "You coming?"

Judy was looking at her with a blank smile.

"Yes, I'm just…I'll be right out." She gestured in the direction of the rest rooms.

He nodded and went out the front door.

"He's so cute, isn't he?" Judy said, gazing after Luke with what could only be characterized as moon eyes.

"What, Luke?" Grace pursed her lips as if she'd never thought of it before. "I don't know, I guess he's attractive enough."

"Attractive *enough?* You should see how the mothers here act around him." She sighed. "Everyone goes all googly when he's around."

"I can imagine," Grace said, not having to imagine since Judy had just gone "all googly" herself. Suddenly, it seemed unbearably hot in the lobby.

"He's hunkalicious," Judy concluded with a knowing nod. "And I happen to know he's got *quite* the incredible bod, though I'll leave it to your imagination just *how* I know." She giggled like an infant.

Grace didn't want to hear any more about Luke's body or what Judy knew about it. She just wanted to cool off and get out of there. "Excuse me," she said curtly, hurrying off to the rest room.

When she got there, she felt as if she'd been hurled back in time. Not only did the bathroom *look* the same as it had two decades before, with the slight exception that the stalls seemed a lot smaller, but it *smelled* the same. They must have a closet full of some sort of School Bathroom Cleaner that smelled of a mixture of medicine and flowers. With a particularly noxious note that Grace had never been able to identify.

For a moment she stood in the cool chrome and porcelain room, letting memories of happy, innocent childhood years swirl around her. She could remember standing in front of this very mirror examining her new braces while Luanne Diamond had tried to assure her that they were "barely noticeable."

The face that looked back at her from the mirror now was quite different. She looked old, she thought, studying the lines under her eyes in the mirror under the unkind glow of the fluorescent lighting. She looked old and tired. Plus, her hair had gone about three shades darker when Jimmy was born, so now it was a muddy, dishwater blond instead of the pale gold people used to compliment her on.

She took her baseball hat off, splashed cold water on her face, then stepped back and tucked her white camp shirt into her shorts, then yanked it out again. That was another thing. She'd put on about twenty pounds over the past ten years, a fact that was painfully obvious in this particular outfit.

Judy, on the other hand, probably weighed half of what Grace did, she thought cynically.

She gave her face a final splash of cool water, straightened herself up and waved goodbye to the ghosts of her past who were still talking about braces, brushing pale hair and looking forward to Santa Claus at Christmas.

She was, she realized, still that kid. And she was still the teenager she'd grown into, and the young wife and mother.

Yet of all the people she'd been and all the things she'd done and cared about throughout her past, there was only one thing she truly regretted. One person she wished she'd gotten to know under other circumstances.

But there was no point in thinking about that now. His ideas about her were set in stone. There would be no changing his mind.

She went outside through the back door so she didn't have to pass Judy again, lest the receptionist should want to elaborate upon her possibly intimate knowledge of Luke.

The muggy heat hit Grace in the face like a wet washcloth. As unhappy as she was with the way she looked now, she didn't even want to *think* how she was going to look after an hour of riding around in that sweltering tin box.

When she rounded the corner of the garage, she saw that Luke had pulled his large old sport utility in front of the bus and had jumper cables running between the two.

"Okay, press the accelerator really gently," he said to someone in his car.

There was an answering growl from the engine; then, to her shock, Grace heard Jimmy ask, "Is that good?"

"Perfect," Luke said.

Instinctively, Grace stepped back into the shadow of the building and watched.

"Should I keep doing it?" Jimmy called.

Grace heard the mixture of pride and excitement in his voice and wondered when was the last time that she'd heard that? She couldn't even remember. That particular brand of joy had certainly been absent since Michael's abrupt departure. And furthermore she had to admit, she'd never seen him display it when he was *with* Michael. It was more like he'd lost a sense of security because his parents had split up and he'd left home than that he particularly missed or needed his father.

The truth was, occasionally when Michael called to speak with him, Jimmy had been abrupt, more eager to get back to a game or television show than to talk with him.

Which was good, since Michael called so rarely.

"Yup, keep accelerating," Luke said. "Hold it till I tell you to stop."

"Can I drive it after this?"

"No."

"Just, like, ten feet? To the end of the parking lot?"

"No."

Grace smiled to herself.

"Okay, ease up on the gas," Luke said, and the engine idle went down. He worked quickly to unclamp the cables from both vehicles, and Grace watched the way his "incredible bod" moved under the thin cotton of his shirt. It wasn't bad, she had to concede. She might, under other circumstances, have dubbed it "incredible" herself. If she was the kind of person to say that kind of thing. Which she wasn't. Still, he looked fit. The years had been really good to him. He'd filled out well, from the slight, wiry kid he'd been to a broad, muscular man. There didn't appear to be any paunch on him. She thought of the post-baby pouch of her own abdomen, which, on bad days, looked like dough that had risen and collapsed.

No doubt about it, time was more charitable to men than to women.

As was the heat. His tanned face gleamed like gold despite—or maybe even because of—his perspiration, and the sweat stains that formed under his arms looked masculine, as opposed to the hideous drenching she was bound to have in an hour.

"Is it ready to go?" Jimmy asked, popping out of the SUV like a jack-in-the-box.

"It's ready," Luke said. "You gonna go with your mom and help her out?"

"I could stay and help you, if you wanted," Jimmy said hopefully.

Luke smiled and ruffled Jimmy's hair. "No way, pal, your mom needs a man along with her in case there's any trouble."

Jimmy beamed and straightened his back.

"What kind of trouble are you anticipating?" Grace asked, coming out of the shadows. "Automotive failure or human?"

"I'd like to be ready in any event."

She gestured toward the bus. "It was the battery?"

"Yup."

"I thought it would crank if it was the battery."

"Not necessarily."

She sighed. The *battery.* For heaven's sake, she could have handled this one on her own. Of course, she still would have been late on the bus run, but at least she wouldn't look like such a ninny.

"Mom!" Jimmy came running over to her. "I got

to help fix the bus. I was practically driving Mr. Stewart's car.''

''Boy, I wish you could,'' she said.

''I'm going to, when I grow up. I'm going to be a bus driver.''

Grace didn't think before she spoke. ''I think you can do a *little* better than that, honey.'' The moment the words were out of her mouth, she remembered Luke telling her he'd done it for five years. Her face went hot.

One look at Luke told her he'd registered her words exactly as she'd feared.

She tried to laugh. ''I mean, if you're going to drive a bus, make it a big metro bus like in the city. That way, you'll get to meet new people every day.'' It was a lame attempt at a cover-up, and both she and Luke knew it.

Jimmy, on the other hand, thought it was a great idea. ''Yeah, that would be *fun!*''

''Okay, get in if you're going,'' Luke said to him.

Jimmy scampered inside and Grace followed. As she passed Luke, she said, ''I didn't mean it the way you think.''

He didn't pretend not to know what she was talking about. ''Don't worry about it.''

Somehow that made her worry even more, but she didn't push it.

''Good luck,'' Luke said as she climbed into the driver's seat.

''Thanks.'' She shut the door and the bus rumbled to life as she put it in gear. She watched Luke as she drove past him, but he didn't look back. He just walked back into the main building, with that confident gait she remembered so well from high school.

"He's really great," Jimmy enthused, apparently watching Luke too. "I like him."

"Good."

"Do you like him?"

"Sure I do."

"You don't look like it. You get all funny when he's around."

"Funny how?"

Jimmy shrugged. "I dunno. Quiet, sort of. You blush a lot."

"I do not."

"You do!"

"It's the heat, Jimmy, haven't you noticed it's like a thousand degrees out?" If she hadn't blushed before, she was certainly blushing now.

"I guess." A moment passed. "Does *Dad* like him?"

Grace took a short breath. "Luke?"

Jimmy laughed. "Yeah, who else are we talking about?"

"He and your dad used to be the best of friends in high school."

"*Used* to be?" He didn't miss a thing. "Aren't they friends anymore?"

"They haven't seen each other in a long time," Grace hedged. "So I guess you could say they just don't know each other very well now."

"But did something *happen* that made them stop being friends?" Jimmy persisted.

Something had happened all right. *Grace* had happened.

"People just move on," she said, justifying the lie because, it was true, sometimes people *did* just move on.

"Like we did. We moved out of New Jersey."

"Exactly. Dad moved up North and left his friends in Blue Moon Bay behind. Just like you moved to Blue Moon Bay and left some friends in New Jersey behind. But Dad made new friends when he moved, and you will too."

"I hope so," Jimmy said, mercifully leaving the subject of Michael, Luke and Grace. "Because it's pretty boring here so far. Except for Tonto. He'll go with us when we move next year, right?"

Suddenly moving seemed overwhelming. Thank goodness it was still a few months away. "He'll go with us wherever we go," she promised Jimmy.

She drove on through town, pointing out her old haunts to Jimmy as they went along. Her list of pick-ups consisted of ten children, and everything went along uneventfully until they were almost back at the school.

Grace had noticed that no one sat with little Billy Spangler, a sweet-faced second-grader with a halo of white hair and the most vivid blue eyes Grace had ever seen. It made her heart ache to see him sitting there all alone, with no one in the seat in front of or behind him, even though four kids had gotten on the bus after him and, presumably, knew him.

She wanted to say something but couldn't think of anything that would get the other kids to be friendly to Billy without embarrassing him in the process.

She had just decided to talk to the first five kids when she picked them up the next day, when a roar of kid voices rose in "Uuughs" behind her.

"What's the matter?" Grace said, glancing in the rearview mirror at the children who were all looking at Billy with disgust.

"Billy threw up."

Grace's heart immediately went out to the little boy. Throwing up was bad enough, but to do it in front of a bunch of schoolmates had to make it ten times worse. "Oh, honey, are you all right?" she asked Billy, pulling the bus over to the side of the road.

He didn't answer.

Grace parked and dropped the keys into her pocket and started back to the boy, when she remembered the Bodily Fluid Clean-up Kit. She'd never actually seen what was inside it, but it probably had something that would be helpful, so she went back and got it then went to Billy.

Fortunately the mess wasn't as bad as it could have been, but the expression of fear and humiliation on the boy's face was worse than she'd imagined. "That's the worst feeling, isn't it?" she said. "Here, let's take that shirt off. It's so hot in here, it will probably feel good."

"Hey, can I take my shirt off too?" the fifth-grader, Eric Bond, asked. "It's so hot in here."

"No," Grace said, then reconsidered. No matter how fun she tried to make it sound, Billy probably wouldn't enjoy being the only kid on the bus who was half naked, especially not on top of having gotten sick in front of everyone. "Yes," she said. "Anyone who wants to can take their shirt off. This is a special deal, today only."

"All *right*." There were whoops and hollers as the clothing went flying. Even little Sally Berger took her blouse off and sat, apparently unselfconscious, in a cotton undershirt. The other girl on the bus, Belinda Wentworth, was in sixth grade and didn't budge.

Grace met her eyes and they smiled at each other.

''I think I'll leave mine on too,'' Grace said with a quick wink. ''I'd rather brave the heat.''

Belinda laughed.

Jimmy hesitated, as Grace figured he would. Where he came from, kids didn't get all excited about taking their clothes off on the school bus. But Grace gave him a look and a slight nod toward Billy.

He understood and gave her a small nod back before adding his voice to the throng.

Grace finished cleaning Billy up and dropped his messy shirt into a plastic bag. Fortunately the rest of the kids were so busy stripping that they didn't pay attention to the process, and by the time Grace began driving again, the event seemed all but forgotten. Even Billy had smiled when Grace suggested he sit up front, close to her. She figured he was less likely to get car-sick there.

She pulled the bus into the school lot almost an hour after classes had begun. It was a relief to see that no one was outside waiting for them. She stopped under a shady tree and let everyone off.

She was calling, ''Time to put your shirts back on,'' just as Luke walked up to them.

Chapter Eight

"I can explain," Grace said, before he could accuse her of any weird doings. "You see, one of the kids got sick—"

"Billy Spangler?"

She frowned. "Yes, how did you know?"

"Happens a lot."

"Thanks for the advance warning," she said. "Anyway, I didn't want Billy sitting there in his messy shirt—it's in here, by the way," she held up the plastic bag, "so I suggested he take it off. When the other kids thought that looked like a cool idea, especially since the bus was so *hot,* I told them they could all take their shirts off, but just this once."

"You did."

"I did." She noticed Billy making his way down the steps toward them and lowered her voice. "And I'm sorry if that makes you mad, but I couldn't just let that poor child sit there alone, half naked and humiliated.''

Luke's gaze shifted to the child as he approached. "Hey, Billy. Why don't you go on in and ask Miss Flynn for one of your shirts, okay?"

"Okay, Mr. Stewart." Billy's voice was so small it could barely be heard.

Grace's heart ached as she watched the little boy pick his way across the parking lot to go inside. He was brave, she thought, the way he carried on and went into school. No tears, no pleading to call his mother and go home...none of the things Grace imagined she would have done if she had been in the same situation twenty years ago.

When he'd gone, Luke looked back at Grace. "You did the right thing."

She was taken aback. "Thanks."

He gave a short nod. "I just hope Ginger Anderson doesn't find out about it."

"Ginger Anderson?" Grace repeated blankly.

"One of our financial supporters. Along with Daphne Silvers, who has refused her support this year, Ginger hates even the slightest whiff of scandal."

"Oh, yeah. You and Fred Bailey were talking about that the other day. But, come on, surely no one would characterize this as *scandal!*"

Suddenly Luke looked tired. Clearly, the politics that went along with his job were more than he'd bargained for. "You just never know with some of these people. And, unfortunately, we have to please them or run the risk of losing support to the extent that we have to close down."

That much Grace understood. Apart from the obvious problems for students and teachers if the school closed down, she would also be out a job, and she didn't want that.

"Got it," she said to Luke, with a mock salute. "There won't be even the smallest hint of impropriety on the bus."

"There'd better not be," he answered, sounding ominous. "We honestly can't afford it."

I'm Too Sexy for My Car.

Grace stood back, with what felt like rocks in her stomach, and looked at the ugly black spray-painted words across the back of the bus.

Who had done this? *Why* would anyone do this? Small children rode this bus, for Pete's sake, children on their way to school! What kind of jerk would emblazon such an obnoxious and suggestive thing on the back of a school bus?

She used to like that song.

"What does it mean?" Jimmy asked, standing beside her and assessing the damage. "I mean, I understand what it means, but why would someone put it there?"

She turned to him and put her hands on his shoulders. "Because, Jimmy, the world is full of jerks. I wanted to protect you from this basic truth for as long as possible, but I just can't anymore. This—" she gestured broadly toward the bus "—is the last straw."

"I guess I better go get Mr. Stewart," Jimmy said, turning toward the school.

She caught him by the arm. "Oh, no, you don't. We're not going to go running off to him every time we have a little problem. Absolutely not."

"But we haven't had any trouble since the first day of school, and that was like four weeks ago."

"Four short weeks."

"We have to tell *someone*, don't we?"

"I suppose we do." Grace pictured herself driving around town, plucking children from their protective parents, with I'm Too Sexy for My Car emblazoned across the back of the bus. Then she pictured herself stopping at a light in town and having Daphne Silvers or Ginger Anderson pull up behind her. It was only a short hop, then, to picturing herself in Luke's office, being unceremoniously fired and handed Jimmy's transcripts.

"I just don't want to have to go running to Luke with every little thing," she said, more to herself than to Jimmy.

"Who else is there?"

That was the question. "Let me think about it a minute."

"What about Miss Flynn?"

Miss Flynn. Grace gritted her teeth. All she needed was to have *Miss Flynn* come out here and survey the damage, tapping her perfectly adorable little chin before going inside and pulling Luke out, perhaps by his belt buckle, which she'd intimated she'd had some experience with.

The only thing worse than standing here with Luke trying to figure out what to do would be standing here with Luke *and* Judy Flynn trying to figure out what to do.

Judy was too sexy for this bus.

"Get Luke," Grace said, through her teeth.

"All right," Jimmy chirped. Since he'd been given the chance to help jump-start the bus, Jimmy had become Luke's number-one fan. Any opportunity to see him, talk to him, or even talk *about* him, thrilled Jimmy.

He ran off to Luke's office, taking a shortcut next to the parking lot. Little clouds of dirt lifted where his feet clomped on the hard earth until he disappeared into the building.

Something like dread lodged in the pit of Grace's stomach.

She waited for Jimmy and Luke by the bus and noticed two locusts caught in the wiper blades. She found a stick to knock them out and muttered, "I *hate* these things" as they thunked to the ground. She remembered the last locust summer, seventeen years ago, and how they'd seemed to be *everywhere*. Dead ones, live ones, you could barely tell the difference because they were so large and clumsy.

These particular two were alive and rose from the ground as soon as they hit. Grace stepped back, out of their path, then went into the garage and tried to find something to clean the graffiti off with. She came up with a rag and some soapy water.

By the time Jimmy got back with Luke, the word *sexy*—which she'd chosen to obliterate first—was very clean, and more pronounced than ever.

Luke took one look at the lettering and muttered an oath. Immediately, he looked at Jimmy and said, "Sorry. You didn't hear that."

"That's okay. I didn't hear Mom say it earlier either."

Luke looked at Grace and shook his head, but there was a small smile playing on his mouth. He tried to scrape some of the paint away. It didn't work. "Completely dry. I guess you're going to have to go with it like this, and we can get it cleaned off later."

"Oh, come on, Luke, I can't drive around like this!"

"What do you suggest?"

"I could take my car."

"And do what, eight runs back and forth? You can't put the kids in the front, and the back seat of your car only holds a couple of people."

"Okay, how about *your* car?" His SUV would probably hold four or five kids in the back.

He shook his head. "Only one seat belt." He gave the back door of the bus a thump with his hand and said, "Sorry. We've got no choice."

"What if Daphne Silvers or Ginger Anderson is out there somewhere and sees this?"

"Oh, I have no doubt that they'll at least hear about it."

"Isn't that worse than getting the kids here a little late?"

"Grace, I can't start sacrificing the kids' education by having them miss class just because I'm worried we won't get money from a couple of prudish old biddies."

"Well, if you put it *that* way, yeah, but will it really make that much difference if the kids are a *little* late one day?"

"Look," his expression softened, "I know this is embarrassing, but you've got to do it."

There was no arguing with him. "All right, I will. I'm not embarrassed." She tossed the keys into the air, caught them, thank God, and cocked her head at Jimmy. "Come on, kid. We've got a job to do."

Jimmy hung back. "Can I just wait here this morning? I...have a little bit of work to catch up on...in the classroom."

"Fine," she said, taking a step onto the running

board and looking back. "That's just fine. Traitor."
She raised an eyebrow at Luke. "You know, a real man
would volunteer to take over the route this morning."

He nodded solemnly. "That's what I'd hoped initially, too, but none of them applied for the job."

"Don't you want it?" stupid Buddy Reese asked,
holding a stick with a locust on the end in Jimmy's
face. Thousands, maybe millions, of them buzzed in
the distance, probably getting ready to swarm. "What
are you, *scared?*"

"*I'm not scared!*" Jimmy shouted, in a voice that
sounded younger than his own, but he took a step back.
He *hated* the locusts. Loud, buzzing, stupid bugs that
flew into your hair and your shirt, and even your
mouth, if you weren't careful. This one had been too
slow to get away from Buddy Reese and his friends,
and now it looked kind of like the shish kabobs his
mother used to put on the grill in the summer, back
when they lived in New Jersey. Back when they lived
with Dad.

Everything was different now, and he hated it. He
hated the locusts and he hated Connor School and he
hated Blue Moon Bay and he wanted to go home.
Whatever hope he'd worked up for the place after his
experience jump-starting the bus with Mr. Stewart had
completely disappeared. He had hoped, when he'd refused to ride the graffiti-marked bus with his mom, that
he would be the only kid in the schoolyard. He didn't
really have any friends yet, and a couple of the kids
weren't all that nice. He knew, even then, that he didn't
want to face guys like Buddy Reese and Corey Wen-
dell alone.

It just wasn't his lucky day. Or his lucky year.

"Look scared to me," Buddy said, waving the awful bug-on-a-stick in Jimmy's face.

"Stop it!" Jimmy cried.

Buddy just laughed. "What's the matter? Isn't your mommy here to protect you? Oh, that's right, your mommy's driving the school bus. What's she gonna do when she gets back? Clean the bathrooms? Work in the kitchen?" Buddy waved the locust in his face again. "Here. Eat this."

"Get away!" Jimmy shouted.

Buddy seemed seven feet tall. "Or else you'll do what?"

Jimmy stood there for a moment, trying to think of what to say or do. Only one solution came to him: He ran.

The sun burned down on him, but he stumbled across the grass as if he were running in the dark. He could hear the boys' shouts of laughter behind him; he knew they weren't following him, but he didn't dare stop or, worse, go back. He just kept running. All the way across the soccer field—even though he knew already that they weren't allowed to go that far during recess—and into the overgrown brush on the other side.

He stopped in the shady depths and stood panting, trying to catch his breath. He was gonna get in so much trouble if anyone found out he'd come here. The teachers had made it really clear where the students were allowed to go and where they weren't. And they weren't allowed here. The thought worried him for a moment—but only for a moment, because then he realized the sound that had been driving him crazy for the past couple of weeks, ever since he'd arrived in Blue Moon Bay—the drone that his grandmother said was the locusts chanting "Pharaoh, pharaoh" from an ancient Egyptian curse—was louder here than anywhere else he'd been.

Tentatively, like a victim in a bad horror movie, he looked around and saw the woods were thick with the bugs. Just in front of him on the ground there were at least four of them, lying stuck on their backs. And there were holes in the ground too. Yuck. Big holes, the size of his finger. That's where the locusts came up. Jimmy's grandmother had told him that too. Every seventeen years they burrowed up through the ground from China and stayed for the summer. Then they went back down again, all the way to China, which was a long way, so it took seventeen years. Egypt must have been on the way, though Jimmy could never quite figure out how.

Suddenly there was a loud hum and something clunked him in the ear, then dropped down into his shirt. Jimmy shouted and fell to the ground, pulling at his shirt until the massive insect fell out. He thought his heart would explode, it was pounding so hard. His breath came out in short puffs, and when he swiped the back of his hand across his forehead, it came away wet. He moved to a sitting position and tried to calm down.

That's when he saw it.

A light breeze moved the leaves above him, and something sparkled momentarily in the sun. When the breeze lifted again, he saw it again. A tiny sparkle in the dirt. Forgetting the locusts for a moment, he brushed aside twigs and dirt and pulled out a ring of some sort. It was really filthy, though. He spit on it and rubbed away the dirt with his shirt.

There was a big green rock on the gold ring, with a couple of clear ones—diamonds, he thought—on either side of it. It looked just like something he'd gotten out of a Cracker Jack box last Christmas, which had been disappointing until he realized he could trade it to a girl for something cool. Mary Ellen Winslow, from his old school, had given him *both* of her Twinkies from her lunch for that ring, and this one was even nicer.

"Watcha doin' here, Jimmy?"

He'd been caught! Jimmy looked up to see that Mr. Stewart was standing over him. Luckily, he looked sort of sympathetic.

"I was on my way back to my office when I saw you running down here," he said, answering Jimmy's unasked question. "Was Buddy picking on you?" He gave a kind smile. His eyes crinkled in the corners, which Jimmy thought made him look like he smiled a lot.

Mr. Stewart and Jimmy's dad had been friends in high school, but it was hard to imagine since Jimmy thought Mr. Stewart looked about ten years younger than his dad.

"Yeah," Jimmy answered, holding back a sudden sniffle. He looked down. "Sorta." There were some small whitish balls on the ground. What the heck were those?

"Come on, bud." Mr. Stewart put his hand down to help Jimmy up. "You're not supposed to be here."

"I didn't really mean to come this far." He bent down and grabbed the two little balls and shoved them in his pocket along with the ring. He'd figure out what they were later.

"Nah, you just ran and found yourself here. I understand." And Jimmy thought he really did. "But you know it's against the rules, don't you?"

"Yes."

"Good. Don't do it again."

"I won't."

"You've got two more weeks, then summer school's out. Then you can have some fun."

"I hope so."

They started walking back toward the school.

"You know," Mr. Stewart said as they walked, "sometimes when a new kid comes to school, the other kids who were there first get jealous and try to act big and tough to let the new kid know who's boss."

"I know who's boss," Jimmy said miserably. "Buddy Reese."

"That's what he wants you to think."

"Yeah, well, I do."

Mr. Stewart looked thoughtful. "You know, your dad used to have the same kind of trouble with Buddy Reese's uncle when they were in junior high."

Jimmy was amazed. His father never told him that kind of thing, ever. *"Really?"*

Mr. Stewart nodded. "Patrick Reese used to wait by the door at school and try to get your dad's lunch money. Then one day your dad decided he'd had enough."

Jimmy's eyes widened. "Did he fight him?"

"Nope. But he acted like he was going to. When Patrick asked for the money, your dad stood up real tall and said no. Know what happened?"

"What?"

"Patrick Reese got scared to death. Backed off and never bothered him again."

They walked a few minutes in silence.

"Think that would work with Buddy?" Jimmy asked at last. "Standing up to him?"

Mr. Stewart shifted his gaze from the sky to Jimmy.

"I think it would. Understand, I don't want you to fight," Mr. Stewart said. "I just don't want you to be scared. Because there's no reason to be. Buddy Reese has been at this school since he was in diapers, and he's bullied a lot of kids, but I've never seen him touch anyone."

"Yeah?"

"Yeah."

"Did anyone else ever bully my dad?"

Mr. Stewart turned the corners of his mouth down and shook his head. "Never. Guys like Buddy and Patrick Reese only act like that with kids who are a little smaller and who seem like they might be afraid. If you don't show them you're afraid, even when you are, they won't bother you."

Jimmy wished his father had told him this six years ago, when Len Malden had picked on him for two years in a row at Tuckerman Elementary School in New Jersey. If Len hadn't moved to Michigan in third grade, he would never have stopped.

Well, Jimmy wasn't going to let that happen again. Mr. Stewart looked like he knew what he was talking about. He was probably right. And if he was wrong…well, Jimmy didn't want to think about that.

They walked past Buddy Reese and his mean friends. Jimmy didn't even look at them. He knew they thought Mr. Stewart was cool so, in a way, that made Jimmy cool, too. He wasn't scared, at least at the moment. He felt the boys' stares as he walked past them, but he just pressed his lips together and kept right on going. They didn't say a word.

It was one of the longest hours of Grace's life. Even when she drove down country lanes with no other traffic, Grace was painfully aware of the message she was sending to everyone behind her.

I'm Too Sexy for My Car.

It was humiliating.

She'd explained the problem to each parent along the route, and they had, for the most part, been sympathetic. None of the kids had refused to enter, although Belinda Wentworth had looked, for all the world, as if she wanted to refuse.

Driving through town had been the worst. Sitting at the light between Bayshore and Magnolia, Grace had noticed one of her mother's bridge partners, Lynn Zook, pull up beside her in a large American luxury car. Grace sank deep into the seat and clutched the steering wheel until her hands were white, praying for the light to change.

It did, eventually, and she returned to the school without incident.

But she wasn't going to go through that again—she didn't care if she had to go to the local hardware store and get yellow paint to paint the bus herself.

As soon as she got back to the school, she marched back into the main office.

"He's busy," Judy Flynn called, just as Grace was about to pound on Luke's door.

By the time Grace turned around, Judy had already scrambled out from behind her desk—and presumably her manicure set—to stop her from entering Luke's office.

"I need to figure out what to do about the bus," Grace said.

Judy slid between Grace and the door and said, "I'll tell him as soon as he's available." She all but waved Grace away with her fingertips.

An argument sprang to the tip of Grace's tongue, but she didn't want to get into a tangle with Judy. "Tell him I'm waiting for him," Grace said firmly. "Outside. And if he doesn't come out soon, I'll come back and wait for him right outside this door."

"Okay, okay." Judy put up her hands. "I'll let him know."

Grace started toward the door, pushed it open and turned back. "What's he doing in there, anyway?" she asked. "Is he meeting with someone?" She wasn't sure what made her stop and ask, but she was certainly sorry she did when she got the answer.

"He's trying to get me a raise," Judy said, with an unselfconscious smile. "He's talking to Mr. Bailey right now."

It took some work not to roll her eyes. "No wonder you didn't want him interrupted," she said under her breath.

"What?"

"Tell him I'm waiting," Grace said again, then exited grandly.

So Luke was getting a raise for his girlfriend, was he? Grace opened the bus door with a yank and flounced down onto the seat.

There wasn't enough money to keep the school running properly, she thought, starting the engine. But there was enough to provide a bit more comfort for the receptionist, who, as near as Grace could tell, did little more than answer phones, flip through magazines and file her nails.

Grace drove the bus up to the gas pump by the garage and jerked it into Park. It was hot out, but that was nothing compared to the heat under her own collar as she thought about Luke and Judy.

On top of everything else, Judy was a good ten or twelve years younger than Luke was. Was he one of those guys who wasn't interested in women his own age? The kind of guy who continued to date twenty-year-olds, no matter how much older *he* got? The kind of guy who would dump a woman who had been supportive and faithful to him for twelve years, even though she wasn't in love with him?

One of those guys…like Michael?

She jammed the gas nozzle into the tank. *Was* Luke like Michael? He never really had been before, even when they were pals in high school. Luke had always seemed…what was the word? He'd always seemed a little less conscious of appearances than Michael was.

But, then, Grace barely knew him. Who was she to say what he was or wasn't like?

It wasn't Grace's problem.

She reached out to stop the gas flow as she pulled the nozzle out, but her timing was slightly off, and gas spilled all over the side of the bus and onto her legs.

"Oh, for—"

"Watch it," a voice came from behind her. "Wouldn't want the kids to hear."

"Luke," she said, then turned around. "Nice of you to pull yourself away to come help me out." The rag she'd used earlier to try to clean the graffiti was still by the garage, and she picked it up to swab the gas off her bare legs.

"You should probably spray off," Luke advised. "Your skin may react otherwise."

Great. That was all she needed. *Reacting skin.* "I'll do that," she said, aware that she sounded snippy but unable to control it. She turned the rag to the bus instead, and cleaned up the gasoline that was still dripping down the side and onto the ground.

It was terrible for the environment, she thought, impatiently pressing the rag against the gas to stop it from running down the side of the bus to the ground. She really should have been more careful.

"So what about the graffiti?" she asked, more disgusted than ever at the sight of it. "I want to get rid of it before the afternoon run, if possible." She gave a half-hearted swipe at it with the rag and turned to Luke, feeling like a sullen teenager. "You think paint thinner would work?"

He was looking at the bus behind her curiously. "How about gas?"

"I just put gas in," she said in an exasperated tone. He knew that, he'd witnessed the whole embarrassing thing.

"No, I mean there." He pointed at the graffiti. It had smeared where she'd touched it with the rag. "Let me see that." He took the rag from her and rubbed some of the lettering off. It disappeared like magic, leaving the paint beneath in perfect condition.

Grace watched for a moment as he worked, quickly and efficiently, his sinewy arms flexing with the effort. It was perfectly clear what Judy saw in him. He was a hunk, no two ways about it. Dark wavy hair that gleamed in the light, movie-star blue eyes, golden skin and the kind of long, lean, muscular body that came naturally to a lucky few.

"Better let me do that," Grace said, reaching for the rag. "You wouldn't want to go back inside stinking of gas fumes."

He didn't let go. "It's okay, Grace, I'm not getting it on me."

She didn't let go either. Their hands were both on the rag, just millimeters apart. "Aren't you supposed to be busy getting a raise for Miss Flynn?"

He drew back, letting go of the rag. "What are you talking about?"

She kept working on the graffiti, without looking at him. "Miss Flynn's raise. The one you were so busy working on when I went to your office that she literally threw herself between me and your door."

He laughed. *Laughed.*

"Something funny?" Grace asked mildly.

"Every month Judy asks for a raise and every month I tell her no. She then insists that I ask the board, *just in case they can find some extra money for her,* so I close the door and pretend to call Fred Bailey. It's a little game we play."

"I'm not sure you're both playing."

"Judy knows assessments come up once a year. She took an assertiveness training course somewhere along the line and got the idea that she should be asking for more more more all the time."

A horrible picture of Judy asking for just that came into Grace's mind. "Nice of you to accommodate her."

"You sound jealous."

Grace's mouth dropped open. "Me? Jealous? Of *Judy?* You've *got* to be kidding. Why should I care what the two of you do after hours? It's certainly none of my business." She was shaking her head indignantly when she noticed Luke was looking at her curiously. "What?"

"Who said anything about Judy and me?"

Grace's face went hot immediately. "Isn't that what you were implying?"

"No, I meant you were jealous of her *job.*"

She wished the ground would just swallow her up, right then and there. "Believe it or not, Luke, I do not covet a receptionist job that's apparently so dull that one needs to pass the time with magazine quizzes on sexuality and filing one's nails."

He cocked his head slightly, his mouth crinkled into a smile. "Interesting that you would think of me when the word *jealousy* came up."

"No, I thought of you when Miss Flynn's name came up."

"Thought of me and felt jealous."

"You've got quite the ego, Mister."

"I know what I heard."

"Maybe, but you don't seem to know what I meant."

He narrowed his eyes, still almost smiling. "Hmm."

"Hmm, what, Luke? You can't seriously think I have the hots for you!"

He studied her for a moment. "No, Grace, of course I don't."

His tone had barely changed, likewise his expression. But something in his answer made Grace feel like a popped balloon. She wanted to reassure him, to take back the insult she knew she'd implied, but what could she say? All she'd end up doing would be to dig herself in deeper.

How could she explain why it bothered her that he took the trouble to *pretend* for Judy? She couldn't even understand it herself.

"Good, because it seems to me that would be highly improper," she said, as if that was what she'd meant all along.

"So what else is new?" He tossed the rag onto a

large rock a few feet away. "Looks like you're good to go."

"Luke, I didn't mean—"

He stopped her with a look. "Enough about it, Grace. It doesn't matter. Just drop it."

Silence shivered between them.

"Okay," she said reluctantly. "Consider it dropped."

He started to leave, then turned back. "One thing I wanted to let you know about. Jimmy's having a little trouble with bullying from Buddy Reese."

"Who's Buddy Reese?" she asked, instantly defensive. Who was picking on her kid? Who would *dare* to pick on her sweet boy after all he'd been through!

"Tall kid," Luke said. "Straight red hair."

"Oh, *him*." She'd noticed him because he stood about a head taller than all the other kids. Initially, she'd felt sorry for him, because he looked sort of awkward.

She didn't feel sorry for him anymore.

"I had a talk with Jimmy about it," Luke said. "I don't think Buddy's going to give him much trouble, but it's something you should be aware of."

Grace was still stuck on the first part. "You had a talk with Jimmy?" She knew she needn't have felt so touched by that fact. It was probably just part of Luke's job to give the kids pep talks under circumstances like these.

Michael had never really had time for that sort of thing.

All of this said even more about Michael than it did about Luke, Grace realized. Still, that Luke had taken the time and the care to speak with her son spoke well of him.

"Buddy didn't hit Jimmy or anything, did he?" If he did, she was ready to fight the kid herself.

"No, nothing like that. He's just trying to establish the pecking order for the new kid. I basically told Jimmy that if he didn't let on he was scared, Buddy would lose interest and leave him alone."

Grace was skeptical. "You think?"

"I'm sure of it," he said, his voice and his expression reassuring. "Don't worry."

"Thanks," she said, emotion tightening her throat. "I appreciate your helping him out."

"Anytime."

Suddenly a locust came out of nowhere, heading straight for Grace's face. Startled, she batted at it and lost her footing, tripping over the gas hose. She tried to stop herself by putting a hand to the bus, but it was still slick from the gas, and she ended up falling right into Luke's arms.

"You okay?" His grip on her was firm.

"Yes." She laughed. "Stupid thing scared the heck out of me." She turned in his arms to face him. "It's okay now."

He didn't let go as she looked into his eyes. She knew he was just surprised too, that he probably didn't even realize he still had hold of her, but she liked the feeling of his warm embrace—such as it was—so much that she didn't immediately free herself.

"Since when are you afraid of anything?" Luke asked softly. "I thought you were never afraid."

She looked at him steadily. "I should have been afraid of a lot *more* things in my life." She reconsidered. "And maybe a few less."

"Really." His gaze was penetrating. It made the

back of her neck tickle. "What were you afraid of, Grace?"

She swallowed hard. This was a moment of truth, the kind life afforded only on rare occasions. It was her chance to tell him something—everything—to tell him the truth about the way she'd once felt about him and the way she'd felt when they'd just gone their separate ways after that one incredible night.

"I was afraid…" she began, looking for the words.

"Of what?" His hands tightened on her arms. It was comfortable. She felt safe in a way that she hadn't for a long time.

She couldn't do it. "I was afraid of a lot of things," she said. "Of not getting into the right school, of staying in Blue Moon Bay for the rest of my life, of winding up alone and lonely…. There's one I'd definitely change. I never should have done *anything* out of fear of ending up alone."

"You never would have ended up alone," he said, releasing her. "There were always ten guys lined up behind Mike."

"That doesn't mean a thing if it's not the *right* guy."

"Yeah, well, you got him."

She scoffed. "I don't think so."

"No?"

She shook her head. "Obviously. And I think maybe I blew my one big chance. I took door number one instead of having the courage to wait for the big prize." She met his eyes for a moment, but felt such a strong sense of…what was it? Loss, or just plain old garden-variety sadness? Whatever it was, she had to look away. "Actually, that's not true. Jimmy's the big prize."

"He's a great kid," Luke said. "You've done a good job with him."

This time she did meet his eyes. "Thank you. That means a lot to me. It's good to know you don't think I'm all bad."

"I never said anything like that."

"You didn't have to *say* it."

He considered her for a moment. "We're just different, you and I."

"Yes. We are. We always have been." She looked into his eyes. "It's a good thing *we* never got together. Isn't it?"

"I don't know."

"You don't?" Her chest tightened.

"Well, I mean, who ever knows what would have happened if things had gone differently in the past?"

She forced a laugh. "Yeah, maybe we would have gotten married and had 2.4 kids and the house with the white picket fence."

"Yeah...maybe." He put a hand out and touched her cheek so briefly that she later wondered if she'd imagined it. "I've got to go back in now."

"Okay." She felt breathless. "Thanks...for helping with the bus, I mean."

"It's all part of my job." He turned and began walking away.

Grace watched, feeling oddly bereft.

Then he stopped.

And came back to her.

Chapter Nine

Luke couldn't say what made him take Grace in his arms and kiss her.

Maybe it was a moment of mental time travel that took him back to a day when her long, tanned legs, sun-streaked hair, and sky-blue eyes had driven him crazy with longing. Maybe that moment of vulnerability she'd shown had been more attractive than he thought.

More likely, it was the heat, addling his brain.

Or maybe—and this was the most likely—it was the challenge in her words.

You can't seriously think I have the hots for you!

No, he couldn't seriously think that. He'd never been able to seriously think that, even years back, when, deep inside, he'd wanted nothing more than to think that.

There was always something that stopped it from

being plausible. If it wasn't the fact that she was dating Michael, it was the fact that she came from the kind of moneyed family that didn't mix with guys like him. Or, now, the fact that she was too sophisticated for this town, this school, and especially this job, and she was going to leave in just a few months, never to look back.

All he *knew* to be true was that he was powerless to stop. Propriety be damned. He held her close, heedless of the fact that he had a position of authority at the school, and that he needed to behave responsibly. With dignity. He needed to be in control at all times.

All of that went out the window. What he really wanted was to pick Grace up and carry her to the back seat of his car, and pull those faded cut-off jeans off her *very* slowly. He wanted to see her bare skin revealed inch by inch as his need for her grew. And her need for him. He wanted to touch her, and to feel her respond to his touch.

He wanted her to ache as much as he did.

He kissed her deeply, holding his hand against the back of her head to draw her closer still.

"Luke," Grace said in a rush of breath, twining her fingers in his hair and pulling him closer. She kissed him hard, and held for a moment before pulling back. "What are we doing?"

"Beats the hell out of me." He kissed her again, cupping her face in his hands. It was true, he didn't know what he was doing. What began as something he felt he had to prove had become something he felt he needed himself. He'd wanted to be the master, but something inside of him bowed to her like a liege.

She trailed her fingers down his back and arched toward him. He felt himself rise against her. Powerless. Desperate. This wasn't what he'd planned at all.

He had to stop. It was long past time to stop.

"Excuse me, Mr. Stewart?"

The youthful voice instantly had the effect of a bucket of ice water on Luke.

Grace jumped back as if she'd been shocked. Then she quickly put a hand to her eye. "I think it's out now," she said to a puzzled Luke, then looked as if she were surprised to see someone else standing there. "Oh, Clifford! I didn't know you were there. Mr. Stewart was just helping me get a gnat out of my eye."

Bemused, Luke turned to see skepticism cross the face of sixth-grader, Clifford Moran.

Grace must have seen it too, because she immediately amended, "Then I lost my footing on the gravel." She slapped her clothes into place. "Thanks for catching me," she said to Luke.

She was a terrible liar.

He couldn't help it, he laughed right out loud, unable to go any further than that with the preposterous story. Clifford Moran was as girl-crazy as they got. Even if he believed Grace's story, which Luke doubted, he was bound to glorify it to something closer to the truth in the retelling.

And there would be retelling.

"What are you doing out of class, Cliff?" he asked the boy, in as menacing a voice as he could muster under the circumstances.

"Ms. Bittner sent me to your office, and Ms. Flynn sent me out here to find you."

"Why did Ms. Bittner send you to my office?"

Clifford's face turned slightly pink. "I don't know, it's totally unfair."

"I'm not feeling real patient right now, Cliff. What'd you do?"

Cliff knew better than to keep hedging. "Okay, she got mad at me for trying to give this to Belinda." He reached into his pocket and produced a ring.

Luke took it and looked at it. It was a gold band with a dingy green stone flanked by two diamond-like stones. The entire thing was encrusted with dirt. Some piece of junk Clifford found in the street no doubt. "What are you going around giving girls rings for?"

Cliff shrugged.

Luke sighed. This was just the kind of thing he didn't want to bother with right now. "All right, where'd you get it?"

Cliff's eyes flicked to Grace then back. He shrugged again. "Found it."

Luke raised an eyebrow. Something in the boy's voice alerted him Cliff was lying. "Is that right? Here at school?"

The boy gave a sullen nod.

"Then you won't mind if I keep it."

He shook his head.

"Look, Clifford, if memory serves, you're not doing all that well in Ms. Bittner's class. Or Mr. Rogan's. Think you might have better things to do than flirt with girls?"

"Maybe."

"Like pay attention to the teachers?"

"I guess."

"Consider this a warning. If you don't get on the ball and start paying attention, the embarrassment of being sent to my office in the middle of class will be nothing compared to the embarrassment of staying back a grade. Heck, you might end up being our first fourteen-year-old sixth-grader. How impressed do you think Belinda would be then?"

Clifford looked horrified, but obviously tried his damndest to keep his voice cool. "I'll do better," he snapped. "Can I go back to class now?"

Luke tossed the ring in the air and caught it. "Sounds like a fine idea. Better hurry, before you miss something critical to your grade."

With one more shy glance in Grace's direction, Clifford turned tail and ran back to the sixth-grade wing.

"Want a ring?" Luke asked wearily, tossing it to her.

She caught it. "Last time I took a ring from a man, it led to disaster."

What the hell was he doing? He should have been doing damage control on the kiss, apologizing, making up some sort of excuse, assuring her it wouldn't happen again. Instead he was giving her a ring.

A cheap, dirty ring, but still a ring.

"Maybe this one's good luck," he said.

Her eyes met his, then she smiled and looked down. "Wasn't good luck for Clifford, was it?"

Or for us, Luke thought grimly.

"Or for us," she said aloud, looking up at him again. "I hope Clifford doesn't go telling tales around the school."

"No one would believe him."

"I hope not," she said, examining the ring. "But you know how kids are, they love to have that kind of gossip. I remember in fourth grade, when Shelly Popadopolis saw Mrs. Little smoking in the teachers' lounge, we all thought it was absolutely scandal—" She stopped. "Luke?"

There was an odd expression on her face.

"What?"

"Luke, this is real."

"What's real?" Was she talking about him, about *them?* What had he done? What had he started?

She looked up at him, and he knew from the look in her eyes that it was nothing to do with romance. "This ring is real."

Normally it would have been a relief to be let off the hook that way, but his tension remained high. "As opposed to imaginary?"

"As opposed to paste. This is a real emerald." She narrowed her eyes and held it up to the light, then looked at him in shock. "A very nice emerald, in fact." Her eyes filled with awe. "Do you have any idea what this is *worth?*"

"No, what?"

She gave a figure that made his mouth drop open. "You've got to be mistaken."

"Look, I may not be able to type or work a computer or fill in a spreadsheet, but *jewelry* I know. And *this*—" she held up the ring "—this is *jewelry.*"

"That's impossible," Luke said, fearing that it wasn't. Fearing that somehow one of his students had gotten hold of valuable—and therefore quite possibly stolen—property. "How would Clifford get something like that?"

"I can't even imagine." She scraped some of the dirt off the stone. "You think it's stolen?"

Luke gave a short, humorless laugh. "I don't think he bought it."

She nodded. "Well, a lot of boys break into cars to steal stereos and stuff and then sell them. It's almost a rite of passage for a certain kind of kid." She raised an eyebrow at Luke. "Which is, of course, *your* area of expertise."

There was no denying it. He and Michael had been

nailed for that very thing once. Of course, the truth of the matter was that it was Michael who insisted he needed a new stereo system for his Mustang convertible, and Luke had gone along trying to talk him out of it, but he hadn't bothered to explain that when Sheriff Gosnell had caught them. After all, it *was* his fault: He was the one who'd told Michael how to get the stereo out of the car.

"Clifford's too young," Luke said, to himself as much as to Grace. "He's only twelve. It'll be years before he even *thinks* of doing anything like that."

"Then maybe he took it from his mom's jewelry box."

"That's probably it." He *hoped* that was it. "I'll give Mary Moran a call and ask her."

"I'm sure that's the explanation."

He heard doubt in her voice, loud and clear. "What?"

"*What* what?"

"Why do you sound like you don't think that's what happened?"

"It's nothing. I'm probably wrong."

"Wrong about *what?*" Sometimes he wanted to just take her in his arms and shake her.

She took a long, thoughtful breath. "Well, this is a really fine piece. A lot of women would keep something like this in a safe-deposit box."

"So? A lot of women would just keep it in a jewelry box at home. Or under the mattress, or in the dresser or whatever."

"That's true," she agreed readily. "But I think *any* woman would take at least some care with something like this, whether she had it at home or stored it at the bank, right?"

"What are you getting at?"

She held it out to him. "The dirt. This thing's a mess. Look at it."

He did. He turned it over in his hand, holding it up to the light and examining every part of it. She was right. It was so crusted with dirt that if she hadn't been around when he took it from Clifford, he might have just thrown it away, thinking it was a cheap old cereal-box prize.

"So it's a mess." He put it in his pocket. "What does that mean?"

"I don't know. But remember when we were in high school and there were some—" she shuddered "—grave robberies over at Highgate Cemetery?"

"Oh, come on, Grace, you think Clifford's a *grave robber?*" God, could he be? No way. Luke dismissed the idea forcefully. Impossible. There had to be another explanation.

"No, no, I'm not saying that. Necessarily. But maybe someone out there is. And maybe somehow Clifford got his hands on some of the loot."

Luke laughed. "The *loot,* Grace? You've been watching too many gangster movies." Inside, he wasn't feeling nearly as light as he pretended he was. "But I should probably call Mary Moran and get to the bottom of this."

"Good idea," Grace agreed. "Let me know what you find out. This is the best mystery I've heard of since *Nancy Drew and The Secret of the Old Clock.*"

A couple of weeks later, the mystery remained cloudy. Clifford Moran's mother hadn't lost a ring and said there was nothing even remotely familiar about the one he'd tried to give Belinda. Likewise, the police hadn't had any robbery reports, and the local insurance company hadn't had any claims filed.

It was starting to look as if they were never going to know where it had come from.

On Saturday the 20th, Grace was up by eight in order to go to the CPR class at the firehouse.

And she was still thinking about Luke.

And that kiss.

And Luke.

The thoughts chased each other around her mind like rats in a maze, with nowhere to go. Yet there they were. She couldn't dismiss them.

Over cold cereal and orange juice, her mother interrupted the cycle by asking, "Are you going to be home tonight, honey?"

It wasn't the first time Grace had heard this voice from her mother. Recently, she'd heard it quite a few times. It was a tone that pretended to be curiosity, but it had another element. It sounded like purpose.

Grace frowned and asked, "Why do you keep asking me if I'm going to be around like you're hoping the answer is going to be no?"

Her mother assumed the pose of someone ready to object, then shrugged her shoulders and sat down at the kitchen table across from Grace. "I suppose it will come out sooner or later anyway."

Grace didn't like the sound of that. "What will come out?"

"I do have...a gentleman caller."

Grace nearly choked on her cereal. "A *boyfriend?* Are you serious?"

Dot furrowed her brow and looked thoroughly insulted. "Is that so hard to imagine?"

"No, of course not. It's just...well, yes, it's hard to

imagine. I mean, all those years with Daddy and then all those years alone. But it's not hard to imagine someone would be interested in you—you're a beautiful, wonderful woman." She was overcompensating, and they both knew it.

"Thank you for the compliment."

"Have you been seeing him long?"

"Just a couple of months."

"So...who is he?"

Dot pursed her lips. "If you don't mind, dear, I'm not prepared to talk about it just yet."

"Oh, my God, is it someone I know?" Grace hadn't even considered that possibility. Who could her mother be dating that she didn't want to name?

Her mother waved a thin white hand. "Call me superstitious, but I just don't want to ruin anything. This is all quite new and...well, as you said, I spent a lot of years alone, and before that I was with your father."

Grace nodded, astounded at this new view of her mother.

Now it was official: Everyone in the world had someone except for Grace.

But she couldn't begrudge her mother the happiness she deserved. "When will I get to meet him?" she asked, taking her mother's hands in hers. "Soon, I hope?"

"Perhaps at the Connor School Silent Auction Ball next month." The silent auction was an annual fundraiser for the school, and the Perigon family—at least Dot Perigon—had gone every year for nearly thirty years.

"Ooh, the ball! How Cinderella-ish." Grace smiled. "This is unbelievable."

"Oh, you stop that." Dot smoothed her skirt. "I've had plenty of dates."

"Not in the past forty-some years, you haven't."

Dot narrowed her eyes briefly. "That makes me sound so old."

"Not old. Wise."

Dot laughed and shook her head. "You haven't answered my question, Gracie—are you going to be home this evening?"

Of course she didn't have plans. She never had plans. The most she ever did on a weekend night was make some microwave popcorn and watch "Nick at Nite" with Jimmy. But she'd been meaning to take him to the boardwalk in Ocean City ever since they'd arrived, and this was the perfect excuse to do it.

"Actually, no. Jimmy and I will be out until…" She raised an eyebrow. "Ten?"

Dot gave a small shake of her head.

"Eleven?"

After a moment's consideration, Dot nodded.

"We'll be out until at least eleven," Grace assured her. "Maybe even later."

The relief on her mother's face was unmistakable. "Oh. Well, if you're sure…"

"Positive." Grace wondered if this was going to become a regular weekend game between the two of them. Maybe they should come up with some sort of signal, like leaving the porch light on or tying pantyhose to the doorknob. "We won't be home until late. But you are planning to stay with Jimmy while I go to this class this morning, right?"

"That's right. I'm going to take him into town and get him better acquainted with the place. Let him see where his mama grew up."

Grace smiled and idly pushed her cereal around in the bowl. "Mom, do you remember Luke Stewart?"

Dot Perigon paused with the coffee pot in one hand and a cup in the other. "Ellen Stewart's boy? Certainly." She clicked her tongue against her teeth and shook her head. "Such a sad story."

"What story?"

"Ellen Stewart's death. Here one day, gone the next."

Grace couldn't believe she'd never heard this before. "How did she die?"

"It was a stroke. Which was peculiar, since she was only forty-eight years old." She handed Grace a cup of coffee. "Such a shame."

Grace shook some creamer into the cup and stirred. She knew Luke's mom had died, of course, but she hadn't realized it was so sudden and tragic. Or that she'd been so young. "Do you happen to remember when this was?"

"As a matter of fact, I do, because it was such a shock to the community. It was all they talked about in bridge club for weeks. Everyone was afraid when they got a headache."

"So when was it?"

Dot thought. "The summer before you started 9th grade."

"I was thirteen," Grace murmured. Which meant Luke had been fourteen. Just a boy still, really. Only two years older than Jimmy was now. "I wonder if that had anything to do with Luke's not going to Stanford."

"Oh, it certainly did. As I recall, he had to stay behind and take care of his father."

"What?"

"Mmm-hmm." Dot stirred some creamer into her own cup of coffee. "Ellen's husband, Ray, had what I suppose you'd have to call a nervous breakdown after her death. Lost his job within a year, nearly lost his house a couple of years later but for the son staying behind and working to keep it all going. Your father even gave Luke some lawn work, as I recall. It was about five years later, I think, that Ray died."

Grace's throat tightened. "I had no idea." Her heart broke for Luke. He'd given up so much to take care of his father. It must have been tremendously difficult to watch his classmates going off to college, knowing that he'd given up the best opportunity of his life in renouncing the scholarship to Stanford.

Even at eighteen, he'd been more of a man than anyone else she knew.

If only she'd known it at the time.

Twenty-five minutes later, Grace was sitting in the clean lecture room at the firehouse. It looked like something out of a 1960s educational movie, with wood-paneled walls, a chalkboard on a swivel stand, and small metal desks. There were ten other people there, most of them middle-aged and none of whom Grace recognized.

Luke was nowhere to be seen.

She hadn't realized she was looking for him until the instructor noted the time and shut the door to begin.

Five minutes into the class, the door opened, and Luke came in. He looked as if he'd just gotten out of bed. A look, Grace noted, that suited him. He gave an embarrassed nod to the instructor, caught Grace's eye and came over to sit next to her.

"Good of you to join us, Mr. Stewart," she whispered with a smile. She was feeling almost dangerously tender toward Luke since her conversation with her mother this morning, but she didn't want to let on.

"Not my fault. My car died down on Sycamore," he whispered back.

"I know what that's like. The bus can't drive five miles without stalling. How about turning some of the budget toward a new one?"

"Pay attention to the instructor," Luke said, gesturing forward. "This is important."

"...so if you'll each find a partner, we'll implement some of the basic principles," the instructor finished.

There was a wave of voices as people—most of whom appeared to have come together—turned to each other and moved off in twos.

Grace and Luke looked at each other awkwardly.

"I guess that leaves us," he said.

"Nicely put."

"Hey, I'm not here to charm you."

"Good thing."

The instructor's reedy voice rose above the murmurs. "One of you will need to act as the victim and one as the rescuer."

"I thought they had dolls for this nowadays," Grace said.

"Not in the Blue Moon Bay budget. Do you want to be the rescuer or the rescued?"

"Oh, the rescued, definitely." She laughed.

"As usual."

"Do you want me to rescue you?" she asked innocently.

He looked uncomfortable and said, "No need."

"Victims, lie on your backs on the floor," the instructor called.

Grace and Luke moved to an empty spot in the corner, and she lay down on the cold linoleum floor while the instructor led them through the motions.

"...now rescuers put a hand on the victim's solar plexus."

Luke put a hand gingerly on Grace's solar plexus. His touch sent shivers through her. It felt so intimate. Was everyone else feeling that way about this exercise? A quick glance around told her they didn't seem to be. The others laughed and chatted as if this were a high-school gym class.

Which was exactly the way she should be approaching this, she decided.

"Is that the right spot?" Luke asked, sounding more tentative than usual.

"I think so," she said, her voice quieter than she'd intended. She cleared her throat. "Yes, that's right."

He continued to follow the instructions, although Grace noticed he also seemed a bit more nervous than the rest of the participants.

When it came time to administer the "kiss of life," Grace's heart nearly stopped. "Does he really expect everyone to do this for real?" she asked.

Luke looked around. "It seems like it."

"You'd think they'd be worried about liability for disease in this day and age."

"Do you have a disease?"

"Well, no."

"Good. Let's get this over with. Here, tilt your head back."

"*You're* supposed to tilt my head back. I'm unconscious, remember?"

"Unconscious people don't talk. Tilt your head back." He slipped his hand under her head and gently tilted it back for her. His touch was warm and comfortable.

"Open the mouth and look for obvious obstructions," the instructor continued.

"Open up," Luke said.

"I'm unconscious."

"Not really."

"Well, I'm supposed to *act* like I am."

"You want me to do *everything?*"

"Hey, I don't make the rules."

Luke rolled his eyes and put a thumb to her chin to open her mouth.

"Ayhing er?" she asked, her mouth open wide.

"No, but it would only take me a second to get a sock off my foot to stuff in there, if you like."

She gave a mock frown. "Luke, I don't think you're taking this very seriously."

"I stopped for a duck crossing the road today by Silver Lake. How many lives do I have to save in one day?"

"You don't get a certificate for not running a duck over."

"And now it's time," the instructor announced, "for the breath of life."

Luke and Grace exchanged looks.

"Still want to do everything he says?" Luke asked quietly.

Her breath was shallow. "We have to," she whispered.

"Okay." He still had one hand under her head but he didn't seem to know what to do with the other one. Eventually, he rested it lightly on her throat. "Okay?"

She nodded mutely, and felt her heart pound in response to his touch.

"Make sure the head is tilted back, opening the airway..."

Luke moved his hand, accidentally pulling a strand of her hair.

"Ouch!"

"Sorry."

"You're not very good at this."

"Neither are you. But then, you've never been a very good victim."

"Is that an insult or a compliment?"

"I'm not sure." He smiled the rakish smile that always made Grace's stomach feel like jelly. "Now shut up and let me save you."

The way he looked into her eyes made her breath catch in her throat. "Okay."

"This is where you'd put your mouth to the victim's," the instructor droned, "but we'll just simulate that today..."

Luke tuned out at the word "mouth." Just the idea of touching his mouth to Grace's fuzzed his brain. Taking a short breath, he looked into her eyes. "Ready?" he asked.

"Yes." She held her breath expectantly, then swallowed hard. "I think so."

He lowered his mouth to hers and the world turned upside down.

A moment earlier, Grace had been aware of the people around them, the cold floor and the bright lights, but the moment Luke's lips touched hers, she closed her eyes and all of that fell away. All she was aware of, all she cared about, was the feel of his mouth on hers, the light parting of their lips, the tentative mingling of tongues. Every movement was tiny. They were like lovers in the shadows, afraid of getting caught.

The pressure of Luke's hand on her chest increased, and she raised her own hand, touching her fingertips to his. She felt as if she might explode.

"And that should do it," the instructor said from across the room. "Stop."

Chapter Ten

Luke drew back and Grace held his gaze for a moment before glancing around to see if anyone—or maybe everyone—had seen them.

No one was paying the least bit of attention to them, and Grace let out a small sigh of relief before realizing that she had bigger problems than what *other* people were thinking.

What was *Luke* thinking?

And what, for that matter, was she?

After the class ended, and they had their certification in hand, Grace and Luke walked outside together.

"I'm sorry about…back there." Luke gave a weak gesture toward the building.

What could she say? "Oh, that's okay…" She searched for some justification or disclaimer for her part in it, but came up empty. He'd kissed her and she'd kissed him right back. What's more, she'd liked it. She could have done it for hours. There was no good explanation.

The truth was that it had been a long time since she'd been intimate with someone. And it had been longer than that since she'd wanted to be. There was always excitement in the illicit, Grace rationalized. That was what had attracted her to Luke all those years ago and that was what attracted her—if you could call the occasional loss of judgment "attraction"—to him now.

"It's like we've got our wires crossed," she said. "Maybe that happens to a lot of people in our position."

"Our position?"

Her face grew warm. "Well, you know, people who had maybe a little bit of...of *something* once, then don't see each other for a long time. It's like some sort of bizarre mental confusion."

"Ah. We get together and think we're in high school."

"Exactly," she said, clapping her hands together.

"Hmm."

"So we just have to remember, you know, where we are. That we're not the people we used to be and that life isn't as simple as it used to be."

"Oh, yeah, it used to be real simple."

"Are you kidding? Life used to be a thousand times simpler." That he thought the opposite was telling, but she wasn't sure what to make of it.

"We can probably agree that none of this is simple right now," Luke said. "I'm sorry about what happened in there. And outside the garage the other day. We both know it's inappropriate, and I don't have any excuses for it. But it won't happen again." There was no mistaking the determination in his voice.

There was no arguing with that. As wrapped up as she might have gotten in the moment of the kiss, and as wrapped up as she suspected she could get in going further than that, it wasn't as if a relationship between the two of them could ever go anywhere. She'd already been in one acrimonious long-term relationship; if she'd learned anything at all, she'd learned not to enter into another one. It wasn't worth it.

She knew all of that. So she was really angry with herself when she went ahead and asked, "Inappropriate?"

"Well…yeah. Really inappropriate. We work together."

"Lots of people work together and have relationships. Not that I'm saying we should have a relationship, of course, I'm just wondering why you're so dead set against it. That work excuse just doesn't hold up under scrutiny."

"How about the fact that you're leaving in about ten months? Not that that's the only thing standing in the way, but it's a major obstacle."

"People have long-distance relationships."

"Not forever. Usually, they do it because they're in school or working jobs that will end or something like that. They don't just move hundreds of miles apart and stay romantically involved."

"That's true—usually one of them ends up moving."

"Or staying," Luke said. "Theoretically. In other relationships, not ours, since we don't have one." He paused a moment, then asked, "Would you ever think about staying?"

"No." Her answer came quickly. Too quickly. She couldn't allow herself to waffle on her plans now. She was finally succeeding, for the first time in her life, on her own. She had to prove to herself, and to the rest of the world, that she could do it. "This isn't home anymore. I feel like I'm living in my old doll house. It's really familiar, and comfortable in a way, but I've outgrown it."

"I don't think you ever even gave it a chance."

"What are you talking about? I grew up here. I gave it eighteen years of 'chance.' It doesn't work for me. I need more." It wasn't until after she'd spoken that she realized that maybe he wasn't talking about the town.

They walked the rest of the way to Grace's car in silence. "Can I give you a lift to the service station?" she asked, trying to find some way to put their communication back on track.

He shook his head. "No, thanks." He stopped. "In fact, I think the less time we spend together, the better. Maybe if we limit our contact to school business, we'll be less likely to...argue."

She nodded. "That's probably true."

"And the less likely we are to argue, the less likely we are to make each other miserable." He looked so deeply into her eyes that her breath caught in her throat. "We have a strange connection, Grace. I couldn't begin to tell you why I'm drawn to you, but I do know it's not good for me. For either one of us, for that matter. So let's agree, here and now, to stop it. Forever."

"Forever," Grace echoed, wondering why she suddenly felt as if she'd been sentenced to life imprisonment.

Three days passed with no personal contact between Grace and Luke whatsoever. She didn't even catch a glimpse of him, except for one time when she was leaving the library just as he was coming back to his office from lunch. He looked particularly attractive, she couldn't help but notice, in a crisp white shirt and charcoal pants that hung just right on him.

Of course, nearly everything looked great on him.

Still, Grace couldn't help but wonder if he'd met someone special for lunch. Or if he ever met someone special, for anything.

These were pointless thoughts, she realized. They served only to make her feel ill at ease in Luke's company and ill at ease when he wasn't around.

So the only thing she could do was try not to think about him at all.

Two days later, she had something new to worry about.

She had picked the last child up for the morning run-in when suddenly Billy Spangler cried, "It's stuck!"

They were on a narrow road with no shoulders, so Grace couldn't pull over safely. She glanced at him in the rearview mirror and saw that he had his finger poked in his nostril.

"Billy, what are you doing? What's stuck? And take your finger out of your nose, for Pete's sake."

"The ball is stuck in my nose!" Billy cried, louder. "I have to get it out!"

Grace bit back a frustrated retort. "What ball?"

Billy just cried harder and jammed his finger in his nose.

"Billy, I'm serious, take your finger out of your nose. If something's stuck in there, you're just going to make it worse." She looked in the rearview mirror again and saw that he did remove his finger. "All right, does anyone know what ball Billy's talking about?"

There were shrugs all around.

Jimmy, in particular, looked concerned. Grace was glad to see he was so compassionate.

"Hang on, Billy, we're almost there. I'll take you straight to the nurse."

She did just that, marching him to the health room as soon as they arrived on campus. The nurse, Margaret Deets, was a brisk, gray-haired woman who looked older than she was. There was nothing warm, fuzzy or quirky about her.

"Billy seems to have gotten something stuck in his nose," Grace said, walking the boy in. "Do you have some sort of tweezers or something to use in a case like this?"

"What, exactly, does he have in there?" Margaret asked crisply.

"A white ball," Billy said, holding his thumb and forefinger up to indicate a small size. "I wanted to know what it smelled like."

"A ball, is it?" Margaret looked at Grace as if to ask how on earth she'd let something like this happen under her watch.

Grace shrugged. "I was driving at the time."

"Sit down on the table, Mr. Spangler," the nurse instructed, then took out what looked like a small dental mirror and a long pair of tongs. She peered in his nostril. "Ah. Hold still."

Billy looked fretfully in Grace's direction.

Instinctively, she moved toward him and took his hand. "It'll be all right," she soothed.

"Be still," Margaret snapped at the boy, then carefully inserted the instrument and pulled out what looked like a bead. She dropped the tool and the bead on the table and asked the child, "Is that all or is there more?"

"That's all," Billy said, hanging his head.

"Does it hurt?" Grace asked.

He shook his head.

Margaret got up and scribbled on a small notepad, then ripped the page off and handed it to him. "Go back to class, then. Give this to your teacher."

Billy took the paper and left. Grace nodded her thanks and started to leave when Margaret stopped her.

"Not so fast. We need to make sure this isn't organic."

"Organic?"

"One cannot be too careful these days." She picked up the bead with the tweezers again. "If this is a harmful substance, we could all be in a great deal of trouble."

"It's a bead."

"It *looks* like a bead." The older woman went to the sink and rinsed the bead off with hot water. Afterwards, she dunked it in alcohol, then held it up to the light to examine it. "Well, it doesn't appear to be a pill of any sort."

Grace held back a laugh.

Margaret must have sensed it because she gave her a sharp look and repeated, "One cannot be too careful. You'd do well to remember that."

"Oh, I will."

The nurse looked at the bead, sniffed, and held it out to Grace. "Do you recognize this?"

Grace took it in her hand and gave it a cursory look. "No—" But something about the color, the satiny sheen, caught her eye. "Hang on." She took it over to the window and looked at it more closely. She'd seen this soft rose-white color before. This was no ordinary plastic bead.

"What is it?" the nurse asked, for once sounding more curious than judgmental.

"It's a pearl," Grace said in amazement. "A very fine pearl."

Billy Spangler's first explanation for the pearl was that there was a "money tree" on the campus somewhere.

Luke's first impulse was to ask, "Where can I find it?" The state funding hadn't come through, Daphne Silvers had rescinded her donation and other patrons were threatening to do the same. And now, suddenly, students were showing up with precious jewels, which had to be stolen, a fact that was certain to upset even the more liberal patrons and board members, perhaps to the point of denying further support. It was almost comical.

Almost.

Except, at this rate, the school wasn't going to be able to stay afloat more than one or two more years, tops. So the money tree idea was very appealing. Too bad it was impossible.

After considerable prodding, Luke had gotten Billy to tell him the truth about where he got the pearls (there were three more in his pocket). He'd gotten them from an older boy in exchange for the fruit leather his mother had packed for dessert in his lunch. When Luke asked him why he'd wanted the pearls at all, he'd explained that he didn't, but that the boy had seemed very eager to make the trade and Billy was a little scared to tell him no.

A brief questioning of Clifford Moran revealed a

similar answer. Clifford had traded his marshmallow cookies for the ring. Unlike Billy, though, Clifford was eager to make the trade, since he figured Belinda would be more impressed with jewelry than junk food.

Luke was glad to get the answers from the boys, even while he was disturbed by them. There were a lot of parents who were used to their kids getting into trouble. Buddy Reese's mother, for example, had gotten so used to coming in for last-minute conferences that she'd stopped asking "why?" when she was called and had begun just giving a list of the times she could come in as soon as she heard Judy's voice on the line.

It wasn't going to be that easy this time, Luke feared. This time the kid in question wasn't the usual troublemaker, and his mother wasn't going to feel blasé about it.

Because the student who had provided the jewelry to both Billy and Clifford was Jimmy Bowes.

Grace had two and a half hours between her morning bus run and the midday preschool run, when she had to drive four of the preschoolers home. It was an easy drive, and she was usually back within forty-five minutes, which left her with a couple of hours to kill. So far she'd found that she enjoyed spending those free hours in the school library, where she could read and help students if they needed it.

That's where she was when Judy came looking for her.

"Grace?" she said in a loud stage whisper.

Grace looked around. There was no one else in the room. "Yes?"

"Luke wants to see you pronto." Judy tapped her finger against her lips. "Top-secret stuff."

"Concerning…?"

Judy waited a moment, then, apparently realizing Grace had asked a question, shrugged and said, "I don't know. He wouldn't tell me. But it must be really important, because he told me not to come back until I'd found you."

Grace's first thought was that something was wrong—something had happened to Jimmy, or they were eliminating her job. A thousand grim possibilities raced through her mind as she hurried to Luke's office, heedless of Judy's pleas behind her to "wait up" and "let me tell him you're here."

Grace gave a single knock on Luke's door before opening it and slipping in. She closed it behind her just as Judy was saying something about Luke not liking interruptions.

He was on the phone. He held up a finger to Grace as he said, into the receiver, "Okay, Len, thanks. Let me know if you hear anything at all. You have my home number, too, right? Great. Thanks." He hung up the phone and looked at Grace with an ironic smile. "Come on in, Grace. Don't stand on ceremony here."

"Is something wrong?" she asked, her voice thick with worry. She didn't know why she always had to leap to the worst conclusions, but she did. Her heart hammered in her chest. "What is it?"

His expression softened. "Have a seat."

That sounded bad. She sat— perched, actually—on the chair in front of his desk. "Is it Jimmy?" she asked anxiously. "Has something happened to him? Buddy Reese didn't do anything to him, did he?"

"No, Grace. Calm down. It's about the ring. And the pearl."

She expelled a breath she hadn't realized she'd been

holding. Slowly, her heartbeat returned to normal. "Oh. The big Connor School Mystery. Did you figure it out?"

Luke gave a single nod.

"Well? Where did the stuff come from?"

"From Jimmy."

That didn't make sense. "Jimmy who?"

"Jimmy Bowes, Grace, your son."

She waved the notion away. "Come on. Where on earth would Jimmy get rings and pearls?"

"That's what I'm asking you."

Suddenly this mystery story wasn't so entertaining. She thought of her earlier theories with Clifford Moran. Car break-ins, grave robbing... She'd been quick to come up with those ideas when it was someone else's child, but when it was her own, she was completely blank.

But Luke, she realized with some gratitude, wasn't the kind to throw that in her face.

"I have no idea where he could have gotten those things," Grace said, slowly. "My mother keeps her good jewelry at the bank."

"And you?"

She gave a short laugh. "I had to sell all of mine. After the divorce." In fact, it was the way she'd funded her move to Blue Moon Bay. "So you see, there has to be some sort of mistake."

Luke sighed, as if he'd hoped for an easier explanation himself. "Both Cliff and Billy said they got the things from Jimmy."

Grace frowned. "I'm not calling either one of them liars, but were they absolutely *positive* they knew who they were pointing the finger at? Maybe they have Jimmy confused with someone else."

"Both of them?"

"It could happen," she said, without hope.

Luke shook his head. "All the other kids have been here for a while," he said, then, anticipating her objection, he added, "They had no doubt that Jimmy was the one who gave them the stuff. He traded it for Billy's fruit leather and Cliff's marshmallow cookies."

Well, that cinched it. Jimmy loved junk food. He was always begging Grace to buy it at the grocery store. Chocolate-covered marshmallow cookies were his favorite. She sighed, her shoulders slumping. "Did you talk to Jimmy yet?"

Luke shook his head. "Thought I'd better feel you out first."

"He's a good kid," she said steadily. Defensively.

"I know he is."

"So there must be some sort of good, logical explanation." But what? She knew Jimmy was having trouble adjusting to his new life in Blue Moon Bay. Luke himself had recently told her about the trouble Jimmy was having adjusting to the new kids at school. But was he so troubled, so soon, that he'd resorted to stealing? Just to be liked? She couldn't believe it.

"Let's call him in and ask him," Luke said. "Unless you'd rather speak with him privately."

Grace knew her son. Knew he wouldn't do anything dishonest, no matter what kind of pressure he was under. She wanted Luke to know that about Jimmy too. "Call him in," she said with confidence. "Let's get to the bottom of this."

Luke pressed the intercom on his desk and asked Judy to call Jimmy out of class.

Grace leaned back in the chair and waited.

When Jimmy arrived about five minutes later, he appeared sheepish and self-conscious. He knew he'd been caught for something, Grace could tell. He just wasn't sure what.

How many things could there be?

"Hi, Mom. Mr. Stewart."

"Hey, have a seat, Jimmy," Luke said, pulling a chair away from the wall.

"Am I in trouble?"

Grace was ready to say—in her best Stern Mommy voice—that they didn't know, when Luke said, "Nope. We just want to ask you a couple of questions." He was as calm and nonthreatening as could be.

The total opposite of Michael.

Grace could see her son's small shoulders relax some, but he was clearly still on guard. She felt the same way, she realized with dismay. Michael had grown so critical in the past few years, so short with his family, that they were both constantly bracing themselves for the worst.

Jimmy looked to Grace for reassurance and she smiled. She didn't need to be Stern Mommy yet. Jimmy hadn't lied. He hadn't necessarily done anything wrong.

"Cliff Moran had a ring earlier that he said he got from you," Grace said. "What we need to know now is where you got it."

"A ring?" Jimmy repeated, in a voice she recognized as Jimmy testing the waters to see how much she knew.

Grace narrowed her eyes. "Are those chocolate marshmallow crumbs I see on your shirt?"

Jimmy looked down immediately, his hand poised to brush the crumbs away.

Grace stifled a laugh and Luke raised his eyebrows approvingly.

"The ring, Jimmy," she said. "Where did you get it?"

Knowing he'd been caught, as he'd been caught by Grace a hundred times before, her son smiled sheepishly. "I found it. That's the truth."

"Where?" Luke asked.

"Remember when you found me by the soccer field?" Jimmy asked.

Luke nodded. "Behind the back goal."

"Yeah. They were on the ground there. Tons of them."

"There was jewelry all over the ground?" Grace wanted to believe it, but how could this be true? "Jimmy, that's hard to believe."

"That's the *truth*," he insisted. "Go and look for yourself."

She looked at the clock on the wall. "I don't have time right now. How about if you do the bus run with me and we both go look afterward?"

"But Jenna was going to take me out for pizza and arcade games after school!"

"That was before you started playing Harry Winston."

"Who's Harry Winston?"

Luke laughed behind her.

"Never mind," Grace said through her teeth. "What I meant was, that was before you started divvying out stolen jewelry."

Jimmy's eyes widened. "They were *stolen?*" He turned his pale face from Grace to Luke and back again. "I didn't steal them, honest, I *found* them. I'll take you there right now and you can see for yourselves."

"Okay, okay, calm down, we believe you." It was Luke, sounding cool as a cucumber.

Jimmy looked at him with a mix of gratitude and bewilderment. "You believe me?"

Luke gave a confident nod. "Your mom and I will go check it out this afternoon. See if we can find any more."

"There's more all right," Jimmy said, in a rush of breath. He looked at Grace. "So can I go with Jenna? Please?"

Her heart constricted. There was so little that he looked forward to these days, she couldn't bear to disappoint him. "Well...okay."

"All *right!* Thanks, Mom!"

"But you'd better be telling the truth about this," she hastened to add.

"I am!"

"Was it right there where I saw you?" Luke asked Jimmy.

He nodded eagerly. "Uh-huh. In the clearing. I think there was lots more."

Luke met Grace's eyes. "I'll go take a look."

"I'd like to go with you," she said. With her child in the center of this intrigue, she wanted to be there when it was resolved. She wanted to see for herself that Jimmy was telling the truth and ensure that the mantle of suspicion was lifted from his shoulders.

"It's not necessary for you to come, Grace. And maybe—" he gave her a significant look "—it would be best if you didn't. In light of our conversation after the CPR class."

"But there are extenuating circumstances now," she said. "That doesn't matter, not at the moment. I want to be part of this. Please."

He paused, then said, "I've got a few things I need to get done first. I'll go at four-thirty. If you're back, you can come with me."

That gave her exactly an hour to do the bus run and drop Jimmy at Jenna's. Unfortunately, the bus stalled three times while she was driving it. Each time, she had to pull over, put it in Park, and restart it. Each time, it did restart, thank goodness, but the whole process added about ten minutes to what already seemed an interminable run.

She got back fifteen minutes later than she'd planned, but Luke was still in his office. Judy, thank goodness, was gone, along with the rest of the staff.

Luke had changed his clothes and was wearing faded army-green shorts and a plain white T-shirt. On anyone else the outfit would have looked ordinary, but when Grace saw him, her heart skipped a beat. *Why?* she asked herself. Why did she react like this to him? Had it been so long since she'd had romance in her life that just the sight of a man's strong, tanned legs, powerfully muscular arms and shadowed square jaw sent her hormones flying?

She was as bad as those mechanics with magazine pictures of bikini-clad bimbos on the wall.

"Ready?"

More than ready, apparently, she thought, but said, "Yup."

They walked outside in silence. Dark clouds were gathering overhead, and the heat had become so muggy that the air felt too thick to breathe. They walked up the hill and past the garage and the bus, across the soccer field, and finally into the verdant woods. The hum of locusts grew louder as they moved farther into the woods.

"How on earth did you happen upon Jimmy here?" Grace asked, wiping her forehead with her palm.

"Pure luck. I happened to see him running and knew something was up."

"Thanks for helping him out."

"I hope I did." He stopped and dragged a hand across his hair. It fell into perfectly mussed waves. "I've been wondering if I gave him the best advice."

"To stand up for himself? How could that not be good advice?"

"Under normal circumstances, I wouldn't have any question about it, but that Reese kid can really be a jerk."

Grace laughed at the unexpected criticism of a kid she herself found extremely difficult. She couldn't help but appreciate Luke's frankness. "He's never gotten into fights at school, has he?"

"No, he hasn't. And I'm pretty sure he won't." A hot wind lifted, rustling the leaves. "But I'll keep an eye on the situation."

"I will too." Michael should have been there to help his son, Grace thought angrily. Not that she wanted him around herself. She didn't. As far as she was concerned, the farther away Michael was, the better, but she knew that wasn't best for Jimmy.

"So, is this where he was?" she asked, changing the subject.

"Right around here," Luke said, frowning. "I forgot just how long this expanse of woods is."

"You mean you're not sure where we're supposed to be looking?"

"Not *exactly* sure."

Disappointment surged in Grace. She wanted to clear Jimmy's name. She *needed* to. She wouldn't always be around to protect him, but she was now and, damn it, she was going to do her best. "Maybe I should go and get him."

"No, Grace, come on. Let the kid have some fun." His smile was kind, and his concern for Jimmy shone through, lighting Grace's heart. "I'm sure if there's a money tree around here, the two of us can find it."

She gave a grim smile. "I haven't so far."

In the distance there was the low rumble of thunder.

"Storm's coming," Luke said, looking up at the sky. "We don't have long."

"What do you suppose we're looking for?"

"Anything that sparkles."

"Too bad the sun is behind the clouds. That would help." Grace picked up a thick, dry stick and poked it through the bushes. "Maybe it would be a good idea to wait till dark then use a flashlight. Although I sure don't want to be picking through the woods at night." She realized she was babbling and stopped, looking over at Luke, who was several yards farther away than she'd thought.

"I don't want you picking through the woods at night either." He stopped. "Whoa, what's this?"

Grace looked up.

Luke was standing still, looking down with a strange expression on his face. Then he bent down, out of her sight. When he spoke again, his voice was thick with astonishment.

"Grace, come here! You've got to take a look at this."

Chapter Eleven

"Ooh, did you find it?" she asked, stepping over rocks and twigs to get to him.

"No, but I found something else."

"What?" She reached his side and looked down. The ground was fairly clear of brush, and Grace could clearly see ten or fifteen finger-sized holes. "What are those?"

"From the locusts," Luke said. "They burrowed up from underground."

Grace shuddered. "Creepy. Is *that* what you called me over here for?"

"Don't you think that's kind of cool? They've been under there for seventeen years, then it's like a light goes on and they all come up at once." He looked just like a kid, full of enthusiasm for the more bizarre aspects of nature.

"It's kind of cool. In a disgusting sort of way. Now

can we get back to the task of clearing my son's name of robbery?''

Thunder rolled again, louder, and fat raindrops began to splat around them.

''No one accused him of robbery.''

''Yet.'' Rain hit her arm. ''But if those things are stolen, and he's the one who found them, who do you think they're going to suspect?''

''They haven't been reported stolen. At least not around here.''

Grace stopped and gaped at him. ''How do you know?''

''I've talked to the police. In fact, I was talking to Len Beall when you came in earlier. He said there haven't been any reports of anything more valuable than a bike being stolen in the past year.''

She raised her eyebrows. ''Really?''

''Yeah, so Jimmy and his Hole-in-the-Wall Gang are safe for the moment.''

''Very funny.''

A crack of thunder exploded, making Grace jump.

Luke caught her by the forearm. ''Easy, there. Do I need to sing 'My Favorite Things'?''

She gaped. ''*Could* you? Do you actually *know* that song?''

''Who doesn't?''

''Plenty of people. How do you know it?''

He looked embarrassed. ''My mother watched that movie all the time. I knew all the songs. So did my father. She made us watch it about a hundred times when we got the first VCR.''

All at once Grace got a mental picture of Luke's family, the romantic mother and the indulgent husband who was patient with his wife. And the boy between them, caught between his loner life at school and a warm home life that Grace could never have imagined.

Once upon a time, Grace thought she'd known what made Luke tick.

Now she realized she didn't have a clue.

Thunder crashed overhead. It was closer now.

Luke's mouth drew into a thin line. "That's getting too close for comfort. We'd better go back."

Grace didn't want to leave, but he was right. The rain was coming down harder now. The storm would be right on top of them in a few minutes if they didn't get out of its path.

They ran across the soccer field, but by the time they reached the other side, the rain was torrential.

Grace stopped to catch her breath.

Luke stopped with her. "You all right?"

She nodded. "Out of shape."

Lightning split the sky and illuminated Luke's concerned visage.

"I don't think it's a good idea to rest here, and the main building's at least half a mile away. Let's go in the garage."

She swallowed and took a short breath. "Okay."

Luke took her arm and led her across the small upper parking lot to the back door of the garage but when he tried the door, it was locked.

"Don't you have the key?" Grace asked.

"Not on me."

"Why on earth would anyone lock an old garage in a town where the worst robbery in the past year was a bicycle?"

Luke looked at her, rain splashing on his face and shoulders, and just shook his head. Then he glanced behind her and said, "The bus."

Thunder boomed again. Before she could ask what about the bus, he answered her question.

"We can wait out the storm there, come on." He took her hand and pulled her toward the bus.

They clambered up the steps and sat down on long green bench seats on either side of the aisle. Lightning sizzled overhead, followed by a quick roar of thunder, as if to dare them to come out again.

"Wow, this is some storm," Grace said, turning to look out the window.

The rain fell in sheets, erasing anything more than a few yards away. Water pooled in large puddles already.

"You can't have this much heat without a storm breaking," Luke commented.

She turned back to him and felt a rush of heat herself. The kind of heat that would *definitely* lead to a dangerous storm. "How long do you think it will last?"

"These things always blow over quickly."

She leaned her back against the wall of the bus and stretched her feet across the seat. "Might as well make ourselves at home while we're here, then." She smiled. "Maybe we should sing 'Ninety-Nine Bottles of Beer on the Wall' or play Truth or Dare to pass the time."

He smiled back, a quick slash of white teeth. "Don't even start singing that song."

"Truth or Dare it is, then," she joked.

He leaned back as she had and they faced each other. "Okay, what do you want, truth or dare?"

"Oh, Luke, I was kidding."

"Chicken."

"Dare," she shot back.

He flashed a quick pirate smile. "Dare, huh? Hmm."

He rubbed his chin, then snapped his fingers. "Got it. I dare you to take off your shirt."

She rolled her eyes. "I'm not doing that."

"Hey, it's the only thing I can remember daring girls to do when I played this game," he said.

"Forget it, I'll start. I'm a little more up on the game. Truth or dare?"

"You want me to take off *my* shirt?"

She would have *loved* for him to take his shirt off, but she wasn't about to admit it. "My dares are better than that. Truth or dare?"

"In that case, truth."

"Truth," she repeated, then thought. "How about this— Are you and Judy Flynn an item?"

"No."

Were you ever? she wanted to know. *Do you want to be?* "Anyone else?"

His gaze was sharp. "That's two questions. No fair. It's my turn. Truth or dare?"

"Truth."

"Why did you come back to Blue Moon Bay?"

"Because Michael's divorce lawyer was better than mine. He left me broke."

"Don't you get child support?"

She gave a short laugh. "It's minimal. See, Michael has a good accountant too. If you believed his tax forms, you'd think he made less than I do." She hated this subject, hated thinking about it. "Enough. You got your answer. Two answers. Now it's *my* turn. Truth or dare?"

"Truth."

"Why did you stay in Blue Moon Bay?"

"I like it here. Truth or dare?"

"Wait a minute, wait a minute, you *like* it here? That's *it?*"

He shrugged. "It's home."

She didn't believe that was all there was to it, but she also knew better than to push him. "Would you ever move?"

He grinned. "It's my turn to ask a question. How long are you staying?"

"A year or so. I'm not completely sure."

She tried to read his expression but couldn't.

"That's not long," he said.

"No."

"Make sure you give me enough notice to find another driver."

A small disappointment niggled in the pit of her stomach. But what had she expected? Tearful pleas to stay? Not from Luke. "I've got a question. What's your biggest secret?"

"Dare," he said.

"Bull," she shot back. "You just don't like the question. 'Fess up. What's your biggest secret? Besides the fact that you know the words to 'My Favorite Things,' I mean."

He splayed his arms. "I'm an open book."

She shook her head. "Not so. Everyone's got at least one secret."

"What's yours?"

"No, no, no." She wagged a finger at him. "It's my turn to ask the questions."

"All right, all right. A secret. Let me think."

Rain pelted the tin roof, punctuating the silence between them.

"Oh, come on, it can't be *that* hard to think of one," Grace said after a few minutes.

He looked at her and his eyes looked bluer than they ever had before. "I can only think of one."

Was it those eyes or the tone of his voice that made a shiver run through her? She couldn't say, but suddenly this game didn't feel like such a lark.

"What is it?" she asked, almost afraid of the answer.

He shook his head, eyeing her steadily. "It's a secret."

"You said truth. That means you'll answer the question no matter what."

"I did. I should have remembered that the truth is always much more dangerous than a dare."

She swallowed and said, "This must be a good one. What is it?"

"You already know it."

That threw her. "What do you mean? It's got something to do with me?"

He nodded, keeping his gaze on her. "I suppose. To some degree."

Gooseflesh rose on her skin. "I don't know anything, Luke." She tried to keep her voice light, although she felt anything but. "You're a mystery to me."

"Let's keep it that way, then," he said, standing up. "I think the lightning has stopped."

"No fair," Grace said, getting out of her seat. "You're cheating."

"I never cheat." He pulled the metal arm that released the door, just as there was another clap of thunder. He muttered an expletive, shut the door and turned around, running smack into Grace.

She lost her footing and plopped down onto the driver's seat. "Watch it!"

"I didn't know you were there."

"Where on earth did you think I was?"

"I mean, I didn't know you were *right* there. Are you okay?"

"Fine."

"Here." He reached his arm out to her and she took it and stood up.

For a moment, they stood there, face-to-face, not more than a foot apart.

"What's your secret, Luke?" Grace asked softly, resisting the urge to reach out and run her fingers through his hair. "What's it got to do with me?"

"I don't have a secret," he said, not moving away from her. "I just made that up."

"I don't believe you."

"What's the penalty for lying?" His gaze danced over her face, lingering for a moment on her mouth. They were still only inches apart.

A thrill coursed through Grace. "No one ever plays with you again."

He gave a single nod. "I can live with that." He reached behind her and she almost leaned into him before she realized he was opening the door. "I think it's safe to go outside now."

Safer than staying in here, Grace thought, following him down the steps. She looked at the sky, the dark clouds moving off to the next town. "Should we go back and look some more?"

"Might get muddy."

"I've been muddy before."

"Let's go."

Ten minutes later, they were back in the woods, only this time they were in a different clearing.

"I think this is the place," Luke said slowly, pushing a branch aside. "I'm *sure* this is the place."

Grace drew up next to him. "Do you see anything?"

"Not yet."

"It's not very muddy," she observed. "That's strange."

"The foliage is so thick in here it creates a natural roof." He took a cautious step in. "Lucky for us."

She looked around. Indeed, they were completely isolated from the outside world. "You could do just about anything in here and not be seen."

"That," he said, pointing at her and taking a step backward. "That is why it's a bad idea for us to be here together."

"What? What did I do?"

"You keep putting ideas in my head, saying suggestive things."

"I do not! I wasn't trying to be suggestive."

He shook his head. "It's just…this happens whenever we're together. We can't keep opening that vein. All it's going to do is make us bleed."

His vehemence took her by surprise. "I don't mean to do that."

"Of course not. You never mean to. You never did." He moved toward her and took her roughly by the shoulders. "But you do it all the time, Grace. All the time."

She didn't shake free, but instead stayed in his face, just as he was in hers. "I do what, Luke? This isn't all me, you know. I wasn't the one who instigated things at the firehouse. I didn't start things outside the garage that day." She drew herself up in his grasp. "I also wasn't the one who started things on the Ferris wheel."

"You also didn't stop things. Any of those times.

You never did. You just let this ship crash up against the shore over and over, and even now, when there's nothing there but wreckage, you don't stop.''

"Neither do you!"

He let go of her arms and stepped back. "Yes, I do. As of right now, I do. I'm finished.''

"Me too." Unable to keep her composure under the heat of his gaze, she looked away. When she did, a glimmer on the ground caught her eye. She looked closer and saw another. It was unmistakable. "What's that over there?"

"What? Where?"

"I thought I saw something." She pointed.

"Let me look." She watched as he went where she pointed and bent down and dug around for a moment. When he got up and turned around, he was holding a long strand that looked like it could be some kind of necklace. "Check *this* out," he said, in a reverent whisper.

"What is it?"

"See for yourself." What had looked, from a distance of a couple of feet, like a thin muddy rope was, on closer inspection, a diamond necklace.

Luke looked shocked. "Is it real?"

"I—I can't be sure right now but," she picked away some of the dirt and mud by the clasp and looked closely. "The gold is 18-karat."

Luke gave a low whistle. "If it *is* real, it's worth a fortune. Even I know that."

Grace nodded her agreement, then said, "Jenna's father is a jeweler. Maybe we can get him to come in and appraise this stuff."

"That's assuming it's not stolen property," Luke

said. "Although what else it could be, I can't imagine. These things don't just occur in nature."

"Unfortunately."

"We'd better take a look around for more. That looks like a bunch of pearls right there."

They both got on their knees and crawled around the space, pocketing stones and baubles as they went. "This is unbelievable," Grace breathed. "If these things are real…" She couldn't even fathom it.

After an hour of digging around, they were convinced they'd found everything there was to be found, and they took the collection back to Luke's office to inspect it.

"Looks real to me," Grace pronounced, pulling a diamond choker out of a mug of water they'd brought in for rudimentary cleaning of the items. She laid it out on a paper towel on the desk, next to eight rings, a diamond cufflink, four brooches, two necklaces, a watch and countless pearls. "I can't wait to get it appraised."

"I just want to know where it came from," Luke murmured, turning the watch over in his hand. It was a delicate antique, made of platinum and covered with diamonds. The twelve, three, six and nine were marked by small sapphires. "Though I have a sneaking suspicion."

"You *do?*" Grace asked, amazed. "Where?"

He set the watch down and walked around to the window. "It's crazy. But I think…I wonder if it's the locusts."

"The *locusts?* Those are some pretty well-dressed bugs."

"No, think about it. They come up from underground once every seventeen years. Things come up with them. Things that have been buried.''

The whole idea made Grace feel a little sick. ''Then why aren't graveyards full of stuff every seventeen years?''

He looked at her. ''I'm not saying they can lift coffin lids or bore through solid wood. But dirt's comparatively soft. They burrow upward, and if small things are in their path, it stands to reason they'd get nudged up too.''

''I have to admit it makes sense. Except for one thing.''

''What's that?''

''Who on earth would have buried jewelry by the soccer field?''

He paced a few steps. ''That's the question.'' He stopped at the window. ''It looks like it's been there for a long time. I mean, some of this dirt is really crusted on here.'' He turned to her. ''If someone had just put them there recently, they would have rinsed off more easily.''

''So maybe you should ask the police if they have *any* outstanding claims from a robbery.''

He nodded. ''I did. Nothing came up in the initial investigation, but they're doing a search.''

''What if they don't find anything?''

''Then I suppose the jewelry belongs to the school.''

Grace's eyes widened. ''That would be great, wouldn't it? It would solve a lot of financial problems. Oh!'' She clapped a hand to her mouth. ''Think about it. We could get some publicity about the found treasure and auction it at the ball in three weeks.''

''Whoa, slow down there. First let's see what it's worth and try to figure out who it belongs to.''

"I'll call Jenna's dad right away," Grace said, still excited by her idea. "He's been doing appraisals for years. He knows the jewelry business inside out."

Luke looked at her sharply and, if she wasn't mistaken, there was admiration in his eyes. "Call him," he said.

While Grace arranged a consultation with Vernon Shepherd, Luke went out to Judy's desk and tried to find the number for Carolyn Kelly, the attorney the Connor School kept on retainer.

He flipped through Judy's Rolodex. Judy had made up an elaborate system, which wasn't exactly alphabetical order but resembled it. The files went from A to Z, but whether she alphabetized by last, first or middle name or title seemed arbitrary. He tried all of them, and finally found the number listed under L for Lawyer. He wasn't sure he was going to need to call Carolyn—that depended on what the police said when they finished their search for jewelry claims—but he took the card out of the Rolodex and slipped it into his pocket.

Then he flipped the Rolodex to B, then to F, and dialed Fred Bailey's number. The older man said he would come as soon as he could, probably in an hour or so.

"Luke?" Grace's voice came from the doorway to his office.

"Mr. Shepherd can come over this evening."

Luke set the telephone receiver down and looked at the Minnie Mouse clock Judy kept on her desk. It was already six-thirty. "What time?"

"In about half an hour. I told him to come on over." She came toward him. She almost looked like a student herself, in her faded jean cut-offs and blue T-shirt. ''If you can't stay and meet with him, I'll do it myself and call you later with his opinion.''

''I can wait,'' Luke said wearily. ''Fred Bailey's coming too. But you go on home, Grace. I can't afford to pay you overtime.''

She shook her head. ''I want to know what Mr. Shepherd has to say as much as you do. Maybe more. I'm staying. And you don't have to pay me.''

The silence of the large hallway fell between them, as each realized they were alone together, once again.

With half an hour to kill.

''So this could be a really amazing ball this year,'' Grace said in a strained voice. ''Imagine the possibilities.''

Oh, he was imagining possibilities all right. ''You are coming, I assume,'' he said, in a voice that was a little too hard. ''Staff attendance is required. But you can bring a date.''

She gave a humorless laugh. ''A date, huh? I've had one offer since I got back to town, and it was from Roger Logan—who is, by the way, married.'' She shook her head disgustedly. ''What a dirtbag.''

That caught Luke's interest. ''Maybe he and his wife have an arrangement,'' he said, testing her. ''You know, an open marriage.''

''Meaning what, that he can screw around with other women?''

''Well…yeah. I guess so.''

''And she gets what in exchange for that?''

A nice house in New Jersey, enough money to not have to work. ''I don't know. Financial support. Shopping trips. Whatever.''

''Yuck,'' Grace said, the distaste clear on her face.

''First of all, that you think a woman would submit to such degradation in order to get *shopping trips* or anything financial is shameful. And second, if she does, she deserves what she gets for setting womankind back so many years. And third, if they *do* have an arrangement like that, *I* want nothing to do with it.''

''So you would never do anything like that?''

''God, no. Are you kidding? Would you?''

''Me? No. Never.'' He studied her carefully. She appeared to be absolutely earnest about this. He reached out and touched the thinnest ice. ''So your problems with Michael...they were never that sort. Other women, anything like that.''

''Oh, no,'' she said vehemently. ''That's one thing I can say for him, he didn't do that. I always told him that was the one thing I couldn't live with. I made him promise me that if he ever had even a small amount of interest in another woman, he'd tell me first.'' She shuddered. ''I never wanted to be the poor pitiful wife, the last to find out.''

Luke could hardly contain his surprise. Michael had been so blatant about his indiscretions. How had Grace missed it? How was it that no one here in town had told her about her husband messing around with other women when he came back to visit?

It was because Grace was so far away, both literally and figuratively. The only people in town who kept in contact with her were her mother and Jenna, and neither of them would have known. Michael would have been too discreet for that, at least.

''When Michael left, it wasn't because of someone else,'' she went on. ''It was that there was nothing left between us.'' She shrugged, as if all the pain she might have felt had dulled a long time ago. "He wanted more excitement, I think."

"More excitement?" Luke repeated, wondering what more that idiot Michael could possibly have needed.

"Yes. He wanted an *exotic* existence. I was happy to make a home. I wanted children and PTA meetings and *Goodnight, Moon.*" Her eyes grew sad. "I know I'm not supposed to admit this, but I truly loved being a homemaker and a mother. I spent years hoping we'd have more children. In my heart, I *knew* that not everyone had come to the party yet...but Michael always had a reason to put it off. Eventually I realized we were putting it off for good. And soon after that, the marriage was gone too."

"I'm sorry," was all he could think of to say. He had seriously misjudged her. How stupid could he be, to believe Michael when he said they had an "arrangement," and that it was okay with Grace if he fooled around with other women as long as she had the house and the car and the money? That wasn't like Grace. And somewhere deep inside Luke had known that.

He must have, because he'd never quite lost his feelings for her.

"Don't be sorry." She waved a hand. "That's the way life goes, isn't it? If you put all your eggs in that proverbial one basket, you run the risk of dropping it. I knew I was taking a chance with every year that passed, and I didn't have a skill to fall back on, but I told myself I'd never need it." She shrugged. "I guess I got what I had coming."

"No, you deserved much better," Luke said, hating the inadequacy of his words. "You still do. You're young, Grace, you can still have more kids and that family life you hoped for.''

She looked at him evenly. ''I don't think it exists. At least not for me.''

A knot of emotion tightened Luke's chest. Poor Grace. He wanted to take her in his arms and keep her there. He wanted to fall on his knees and beg her to stay and let him make up for all the damage that had been done to her. To make up for the fact that he'd let her go without a fight when he might have been able to spare her the pain Michael had inflicted time and again, and for the emptiness she felt now that the life she'd expected had slipped through her fingers.

Who knew if she would have stayed with Luke, or even if he could have persuaded her to go out with him one more time back then, but one thing was for sure: It was too late now. Her life had taken her in a different direction and, although she was back in town thanks to an unexpected detour, she fully intended to continue on the path she'd started, as much as she could. And that meant she was going back where it all began for her. She was leaving. There was no stopping her.

And Luke told himself he would have to be a fool to give his heart to her, only to watch her walk away with it.

Again.

Chapter Twelve

Grace had to wonder if there was something Luke wasn't telling her, but she didn't want to ask.

She didn't want to know.

It wasn't that she couldn't bear the possibility of Michael having a relationship with someone else. She had long since grown immune to whatever pain he might inflict. In fact, whatever put more distance between her and their marriage was good, as far as she was concerned.

What she couldn't stand now was the idea that Luke might think she was a fool who had sat at home knitting and believing her husband to be working late when he was really out carousing.

She looked at her watch. Twenty-five minutes before Mr. Shepherd would arrive. What were they going to do?

Luke turned the chair around and leaned back, appraising Grace. "So. What are you going to do with yourself when you get back to New Jersey?"

When he said it, New Jersey sounded like a foreign place. It sounded very far away. It sounded like a place she'd rather not go, and a life that, perhaps, she'd rather not resume.

"I'm going to work for a friend who plans on opening a PR firm," she said decisively. Because she had, after all, made the decision. Neither exhaustion nor sentimentality was reason enough to change her plans. "Believe it or not, my charity work did help lend me the skills for that job."

He steepled his hands in front of him and stared at them. "I'm sure you could do anything you put your mind to."

"Even driving a bus?"

He raised his blue eyes to hers. "Even driving a bus. You've proven that."

Something about his expression made gooseflesh rise on her skin. She rubbed her bare arms. "So you admit you were wrong about me?"

"Oh, yeah," he said, a little quicker than she expected. "I was wrong about you all right. I completely underestimated you and I'm sorry."

"We are talking about the job, aren't we?"

He hesitated. "Yes. The bus. I've got to hand it to you, Grace, I wasn't sure you'd pass the test. Scratch that, I wasn't sure you'd *take* the test, once you saw everything that was involved in this job."

She shrugged. "I told you, I had no choice. Oddly enough, the job has turned out to be more fun than I thought it would be." She smiled and leaned a hip against the desk. "Don't tell anyone, but I'm actually kind of enjoying it."

He lifted his foot and pushed it against her thigh. "Get out of here."

She laughed. "It's true."

"Will wonders never cease? Next thing you know, you'll be telling me that you're going to stay in town instead of moving back to New Jersey, and I'll have to keep you on as a bus driver."

Was it hope she heard in his voice? Or cynicism? Knowing Luke, it was the latter.

"No, Luke, don't worry, you can get yourself a *real* bus driver. I'm going home eventually."

He shook his head but said nothing.

"What?" she asked.

"It's just so strange to hear you say that. You're going home." Idly, he lifted a pencil—a pencil that appeared to have a tiny stuffed animal where the eraser should be—from the desk and turned it in his fingers. "Like you're not home now. Here."

"Well…I'm not. I guess." She threw her hands in the air. "No place feels like home to me anymore."

"Then how do you know where to go?"

She sighed. "Because where we lived in New Jersey feels like home to Jimmy. That's the important thing."

The corners of his mouth turned down. "I don't know. Jimmy seems to be enjoying it here. More and more so. You hear he made Buddy Reese back down?"

Grace gasped. "No! When?"

"This afternoon. In front of a whole bunch of kids." Luke looked proud.

She wanted to kiss him for that.

But she didn't. Instead she said, "What happened?"

Luke's smile was broad. "Jimmy told Buddy to leave him—*and* all the smaller kids Buddy's been picking on—alone, or else he'd use his 'deadly karate' on him. Does Jimmy know karate?''

Grace shook her head in amazement. ''He took two or three lessons once when the local studio offered them for free, but he never wanted to follow through with it.''

Luke laughed. ''I guess he didn't need to. Buddy went white as a sheet and said he'd just been joking with Jimmy, ha ha. Jimmy just had this fierce look on his face.'' Luke imitated the look, then laughed. ''And he kept it there until Buddy put his hands up and walked away.''

''I can't believe it. What did Jimmy do then?''

''He went a little limp,'' Luke admitted. ''Until he saw me. Then he straightened up and gave me the thumbs-up.''

''Well, good for him.'' Grace couldn't have been more delighted for her son, but she was also aware of a growing gratitude toward Luke. It wasn't the first time he'd done what Michael should have but didn't.

''I guess Jimmy's going to tell me about it when he gets home tonight.''

''Oh, this is going to be one of those big stories that keeps on getting bigger. I have a feeling.''

Grace laughed with him. ''It's all thanks to you, you know,'' she said.

He looked down, obviously uncomfortable with her gratitude. ''I didn't do anything.''

''Yes, you did. You gave him confidence and support. You gave him the kind of guy advice he wouldn't take from me, even if I were to try to give it to him. The kind of guy advice a father should give, if he's any kind of father at all. I'm so glad you were there to do that for him.''

"It was nothing." His "aw, shucks" attitude was so genuine it was endearing. "I just wish I could be around him when he gets interested in girls. There are a few things I'd like to warn him about."

"Oh? Like what?"

"Guy stuff."

"Such as…?"

He looked up at her. "For one thing, I'd tell him to avoid women like his mother."

"Like me?" She wasn't sure how to take that. "What's wrong with me?"

"You're a heartbreaker."

"A *heartbreaker!*" A shiver went down her back. "I don't know who gave you that idea."

"That's one I formed on my own."

Her chest tightened. Were they really having this conversation? After all the years that had passed, was she finally hearing how he really felt about her? "Come off it, Luke, I didn't break your heart?" It was a question, not a statement.

He gave her exactly the answer she wanted. The way he looked at her, the way the light gleamed off his wavy dark hair and the way the shadows fell on his face, it was the answer any red-blooded woman in America would have wanted to hear. "Yes, you did. Before that, I didn't even think it was possible. No one else has ever even come close."

Her knees felt weak, but there was no place for her to sit without moving across the room. And she didn't want to move so far away from him.

She wanted to move closer.

But she didn't dare. "That night…that night we met in Ocean City?"

"That night and a hundred others." He drew in a

long breath. "But, yes, that night too. Maybe that night in particular."

She wanted to reach out and take him in her arms. It had been years, but she had hurt him and she wanted to erase all vestiges of the pain her selfishness and fear had caused him. "I was so confused," she said, unsure if there were any words to adequately express how she felt, either then or now. "I didn't know what to do with everything that happened, or with the way I felt about you. It scared me to death."

"Why?"

How could she explain? She didn't understand it all herself. "I—" She threw her hands up and turned away from him, to walk to the window. "I don't know."

He got up and followed her, turning her roughly to face him. *"Why?"* he repeated. "Why did it scare you?"

"Because...because I was afraid you didn't feel the way I felt." There. It was out. She'd admitted to him what she'd never truly even admitted to herself. She met his heated gaze with shame. "I know it's not noble, Luke. But it's the truth. I was so afraid to leave Michael and be alone."

"But you wouldn't have been alone," he said softly.

"I didn't know that. Before that night, all you and I ever did was argue. I knew I was attracted to you, but I had no idea you were attracted to me. When we got together that night—" she shivered, the memory still affecting her "—it was incredible. Like a dream. And I didn't want to change my life only to find out that it *had* been a dream. Or some sort of joke."

He looked as if she'd slapped him. "A *joke?* Did you really think I was like that?"

"No. No, of course not." Michael was. But not

Luke. She'd known that, even then. "But what happened that night wasn't an offer from you, it was a moment of desire. Afterward, I guess what I was really afraid of was that you'd changed your mind. Or that maybe you'd regretted what had happened." She lifted her shoulders half-heartedly. "And maybe you did. I still don't know."

He shook his head slowly. "I didn't regret it. Not for one moment."

Tears welled in her eyes. "You never said anything. I looked for clues, but you didn't give anything away."

"What could I say? I couldn't ask you to leave him. I figured if you didn't do it, it was because you didn't want to. I couldn't *make* you love me."

"You did," she said, in a rush of breath. "I did."

His expression cleared. "You…?"

She nodded. "And I botched the whole thing. I made a terrible mistake." Her voice caught in her throat. "A whole bunch of them."

Luke pulled her into his arms in one fluid movement. For a long time they stood there, locked together in a desperate embrace.

"I should have…tried," Luke said, holding her tight. "Hell, I should have begged you to stay." He pulled back and put his hands on her shoulders, looking deeply into her eyes. "Maybe I should now."

Her throat felt so constricted she could barely speak. "No. Don't. Please. I can't. I just can't."

"Why not?" He dropped his hands in frustration. "Why are you so pigheaded about this? Do you really hate it here that much?"

"No. It's not about me." She put the heels of her hands against her eyes for a moment to stop the tears. "It's Jimmy. So many promises have been broken in his life already. I can't break another one. Especially one that I know is so important to him.'' She took a short breath and raked her hand through her hair, feeling powerless. ''He wants to go home. So I'm going to take him home, by God, no matter what it takes.''

Luke's expression sobered. ''He's a lucky kid to have a mother like you.''

''I don't know if that's true. But I have to do my best for him. It's the most important thing.''

''But what do *you* want?'' Luke asked. ''What do you need?''

''I don't know.'' Maybe the fact that she didn't know, the fact that, after only a few months back in Blue Moon Bay she wasn't so sure she wanted to leave, was an answer in and of itself. ''But if I were going to stay…it doesn't matter. I'm not staying.''

''Another lost opportunity,'' he said softly, then touched her chin. ''Think we'll ever get this right?''

Her eyes burned. ''It doesn't seem like it.''

A long moment passed. He touched her cheek, her chin.

''How about one night?'' she heard herself ask.

''A night? You and me?''

She nodded. The small ember of longing for Luke, which had burned inside her for years, flickered. ''One night so you and I can get this—this *curiosity* we have about each other out of the way.'' She wasn't sure if she was trying to convince him or herself. ''So we don't have to spend the next several months looking sideways at each other, wondering.''

He nodded doubtfully. ''Could work.''

''Ignoring it hasn't.''

''True.'' He smiled. ''When?''

''Tonight.'' Her breathing grew shallow.

He kissed her, long and deep, then asked, "What do you want to do?"

The ember ignited, and her body flamed to life. "Several things come to mind right off the bat."

He gave a sly smile and brushed his fingertips across her lips. "It's been a long time since we started this."

She nodded. "I'll see if Jenna can keep Jimmy and Tonto overnight," she said, her voice barely above a whisper. How could she wait? She wanted to be with him *now*.

He kissed her again.

They would have lost themselves to their desire right then and there, but for the sweep of headlights that crossed the wall from a car in the parking lot outside the window.

"Mr. Shepherd's here," Grace said, reluctantly drawing back from Luke's arms. She lingered for a moment with her fingertips on his arms, then said, "I'd better get the door." She crossed the room, acutely aware of his gaze on her backside, and opened the door for the older man.

Grace hadn't seen him for years, but he looked exactly the same as she remembered. Short and lithe, with salt-and-pepper hair and a bald spot at the crown. His eyes were sharp, and magnified by the square-framed glasses he'd worn for as long as she could remember.

"Mr. Shepherd!" She smiled, hoping to hide her disappointment that he'd managed to be so prompt. "It's so good to see you."

"It's good to see you too, Grace, very good indeed. Jenna has been walking on air ever since she found out you were coming home. We just wish you were staying longer."

"It certainly is tempting," she said, aware of Luke moving behind her.

He went into his office and came out with the file box they'd put the jewelry in.

"This is what we've found so far," Luke said, setting it down. She allowed herself, for once, to enjoy the sight of his powerful arms, flexing with his movements.

For once she could indulge in the pleasure of watching him, because she knew, finally, that those arms would be holding her tonight. She knew she would feel that powerful, lean body on hers. For one short night, the smorgasbord of Luke's assets would be hers to sample freely.

Inside, she was trembling with anticipation.

If Luke felt the same, and she suspected he did, he didn't show it. He was cool as a cucumber, setting the box down and telling Vernon Shepherd about how they'd found the items.

Vernon listened with interest, then went to the box and took a piece out. It was the ring that had started everything. The emerald ring Jimmy had given to Clifford.

"Hmm." Vernon frowned for a moment and took a loupe out of his breast pocket. "Very interesting."

"It's the real deal, isn't it?" Grace said, glancing at Luke.

Judy was right. He was hunkalicious.

Grace nearly laughed but instead forced her concentration back to Luke.

"Oh, indeed, indeed it is." He glanced in the box. "Tell me, did you find a sapphire ring that looks something like this? Emerald-cut, with two diamonds, on a platinum band instead of gold?"

"Yes, as a matter of fact, we did," Grace said, surprised. The ring he described was exquisite, even caked with mud. It had caught her eye as soon as they'd found it. "How on earth did you know?"

"Call it a hunch." Vernon reached into the box and took out a diamond necklace and a choker. He barely glanced at them before nodding and looking up at Luke and Grace. "Mmm-hmm, this is just as I suspected." He took the loupe from his eye and looked from Grace to Luke. "I remember this collection quite well."

Chapter Thirteen

"You *remember* it?" Luke repeated.

Vernon nodded. "I appraised it for insurance purposes about, hmm, twenty years ago now."

"Whose is it?" Grace asked. Her face was flushed with excitement. She looked prettier than Luke had ever seen her.

"Edna Connor's." Vernon chuckled to himself. "And she did *not* want me looking at it, I can tell you that. Sat right there, not two feet away from me, the entire time I evaluated the collection, like she expected me to slip some of the things into my pockets. Truthfully, I think she was a bit dotty."

Dotty was putting it nicely, from what Luke had heard. At the end of her life, Edna Connor appeared to have gone stark, raving mad. She'd hidden all of her money in a hole in her mattress—they'd found that after her death—but unfortunately had grown so mistrustful of the government that she'd failed to pay her last two years' worth of taxes. That had eaten up a considerable percentage of the cash they'd found.

She'd finally been taken out of her home and put into a full-time care facility when she'd begun taking shots at "trespassers" with a pellet gun. Unfortunately, the trespassers in question were the teachers who had come onto the campus in late August to prepare for a new school year.

Fred Bailey—up to then, Edna's closest friend—had somehow persuaded her to give up the gun and go with him to a place that could help her. She'd spent another four years in Highwater House before she died.

"Was she robbed?" Grace asked.

"Not that I'm aware of," Vernon answered. "But, then, they wouldn't have notified me if she was. My part was done when I completed the appraisal."

"But you would have recognized the jewelry if anyone had ever tried to pawn it at your shop, right?" Grace asked.

"Without a doubt. It's an extremely unusual collection. Some pieces are quite rare. Take that platinum-and-sapphire ring we discussed, for example." He took it out of the box and held it up to the light with some reverence. "Ah, yes. A stunning ring. The stone is absolutely perfect." He looked back at Grace. "This was the engagement ring of Princess Mirabelle of Kublenstein. Are you familiar with her story?"

"No," Grace said, looking enchanted. Like a young girl listening to a fairy tale.

In a way that was exactly what she was, Luke realized. She was an idealist who always expected everything to work out, no matter how grim the reality. It was that quality that had allowed her to marry Michael

Bowes, hoping the town perception of them as "the golden couple" would turn out to be true. Despite the fact that, perhaps, her instincts had told her otherwise.

It was also the quality that had allowed her to take a job as a school-bus driver. It wasn't what she wanted to do for the rest of her life, they both knew that from the beginning, but she had believed that if she managed to muddle through this cloudy time in her life, she'd eventually get to the silver lining.

"Princess Mirabelle was a commoner who married the prince of a tiny Alpine country," Vernon told her. "I can't recall his name. Georg, I think. In any event, he'd married her against his parents' wishes, but she charmed the entire country before dying tragically young. Very romantic story." He handed the ring to Grace. "Edna had gone to great trouble to win the ring at auction."

"Did Edna wear it herself?" Grace asked, slipping it onto her finger and holding her hand out to admire it.

Luke noticed she put it on her left hand.

And that it looked good there.

"No, no, it was too large for Edna. She refused to let me size it. She didn't want it changed at all. So I suppose she just kept it." Vernon gave Grace a smile full of fatherly pride. "Seems to fit you just perfectly, Cinderella."

She sighed and took the ring off. "I have a feeling it's out of my price range."

Across the room, the door swung open and Fred Bailey came in.

"Sorry it took me so long to get here," Fred said. "What's this about finding jewelry on the school property?"

"It turns out that it belonged to Edna Connor," Grace chirped.

Luke filled him in on the highlights of the story. "Do you know if Edna was ever robbed?" he asked when he'd finished.

Fred laughed outright. "I'd pity any poor soul who tried to rob that hellcat. No, I suspect the answer to this is a bit simpler. Wouldn't you say, Vernon?"

Vernon Shepherd set down the large brooch he was examining. "Yes, I would indeed."

"What do you mean?" Luke asked. "What do you think the explanation is?"

Fred took his glasses off and rubbed his eyes. "At the end of her life, Edna was…how shall I put it? She wasn't herself anymore. She grew very mistrustful of the government and big business and even the board of directors here at Connor." He gestured at Luke with his glasses. "You probably recall the time she tried to fire everyone."

He did. "I got a pink slip myself that day." At the time, it had amused him to picture little Edna taking over his job as the bus driver.

"What are you saying?" Grace asked. "That she buried the jewelry herself?"

"That's precisely what I'm saying."

Which meant that the entire collection was part of her estate. An estate that had been left to the school.

Which meant that Grace had been right when they found it: the board of trustees could sell it and bring in money to help keep the school operating.

"Do you still have an itemized copy of the appraisal you did?" Fred asked Vernon.

"I have a copy of every appraisal I've ever done," Vernon said, with a satisfied nod. "Particularly ones of this magnitude. The collection was worth well over a million back then.''

The meeting with Vernon Shepherd and Fred Bailey went better than Grace could have imagined.

Vernon took the jewelry with him to clean it up and compare what they'd found to his complete listing of Edna's collection.

Fred had said they'd need to make sure an insurance claim had never been made for the jewels, and they'd have to confer with Edna's estate lawyer, but that it looked as if they'd be able to add them to the silent auction to raise money for the school.

And Luke had told Grace that, yes, if everything else was a go, she could send some press releases to the local and national newspapers to try to work up some additional interest in the auction.

Perhaps most important, while Luke had ironed out the details with Fred Bailey, Grace had slipped into Luke's office and asked Jenna if Jimmy could sleep over.

Jenna was tactful enough not to ask for details about Grace's plans, but she indicated to Grace that she would be more than willing to listen if Grace wanted to talk about it later.

Which meant, of course, that she wanted every single detail as soon as Grace was available to tell all.

''I'll drive,'' Luke said as soon as Fred Bailey's taillights disappeared down the gravel road off the campus. ''We'll get your car in the morning.'' He took her in his arms and kissed her long and hard, leaving her dizzy with desire and anticipation.

The five-minute drive to Luke's house—which

turned out to be a waterfront cabin—might as well have taken an hour for how impatient Grace felt. It took all of her restraint not to tell him to pull the car over on the abandoned country lane and slip into the back seat with her.

But she wanted it to be perfect.

He turned the car off the road and gunned it down a short drive, the tires spitting gravel behind them. A couple of minutes later he drew to a halt outside a surprisingly large wooden cabin with lots of tall windows.

"How long has this place been here?" Grace asked. "I don't remember it."

"That's because I've been building it for the past eight or nine years," Luke said, throwing the door open and hauling Grace out the driver's side.

She giggled and followed him. He kicked the door shut behind her.

"Your keys are in there."

"I'll take my chances," he said, drawing her to him and kissing her hungrily. "That was the longest drive of my life."

"Mine too. And that includes the time I had to drive the bus with I'm Too Sexy for My Car spray-painted on it."

"You are too sexy for that bus," Luke said, leading her through the front door. "Way too sexy."

They headed for the stairs and clambered up to a large bedroom with one wall that was all window. The other three were pale knotty pine. Grace loved it. "Did you do all this yourself?" she asked, amazed.

He started to unbutton her blouse. "Yes. Now, can we stop talking about the house? I'll tell you everything you want to know later. For now—" he peeled the shirt

off her ''—I've got more important things in mind.''
He bent down and kissed her neck, and soon the house
was forgotten completely.

''I've wanted to do this for so long,'' Luke murmured, trailing kisses along her jawline.

She sighed and wrapped her arms around him, unable to form words as spirals of pleasure whirled
through her.

He moved his hands up her back, unfastening her
bra in one smooth move, and slipped the straps off her
shoulders. It dropped to the floor.

Then he moved down slowly, kissing her throat, her
breast bone, her stomach…he knelt before her and,
locking eyes with her, undid the button on her jeans
and slowly dragged the zipper down.

Grace drew in a shuddering breath but stood fast as
he slipped the jeans over her hips.

''You're so beautiful,'' he said to her.

''I'm so naked,'' she said with a small laugh as she
stepped out of the pant-legs. ''And you're not.''

His smile was wicked. ''Hard to say who's got the
better deal here,'' he said, hooking a finger over the
front of her panties and, with one small tug, pulling
them off her. ''I think it's me.''

Her knees went weak.

As if he sensed that, he gently lifted her and carried
her to the wide, plush bed. ''You need to relax,'' he
said, his voice thick with passion. ''Let me take care
of you.''

When was the last time a man had said that to her?
Had a man *ever* said that to her?

She relaxed against the soft pillows as Luke returned
his attention to her, working his mouth and his hands

slowly down her body until she thought she might go mad.

She tried to swallow, to compose herself, but as soon as he parted her thighs, she was gone. What she remembered of his touch from seventeen years ago was a mere shadow of the skill he possessed now. He played her like a harp, touching every string, playing tunes she didn't even know.

It was bliss. He touched her in ways that no one ever had, bringing her to the brink of ecstasy over and over, then artfully backing away, letting the pleasure linger in little shivers of desire.

When she couldn't stand it any longer, she said, ''I want you.'' She pulled at his shirt and, with his help, pulled it over his head.

Together they fumbled at his jeans, laughing nervously, until at last they were skin to skin.

''I need you,'' Grace said. ''I need you now. We've waited way too long.''

He didn't ask questions. He didn't have to. As if he was able to read every nuance of her desire, he moved his weight on top of her, entering her with a quick, satisfying thrust.

Grace gasped, then sighed and relaxed in his strong embrace as he moved within her. This, she realized for the first time in her life, was what lovemaking was supposed to be. This was what it was all about.

They were as one. It wasn't just her body that he stroked, it was her soul. This experience wasn't merely physical, it was almost spiritual. She felt as if she'd never breathed before now. Slowly their fervor increased, until everything within her exploded in a volcano of sensations which melted over her like hot lava.

And as she shuddered with the aftershocks of her

climax, he reached his own, breathing harshly against her neck until, with one final and powerful thrust, he exhaled explosively and dropped his head to her neck, shuddering with release, then took her in his arms again and rolled them so they lay entwined in a tumult of blankets and pillows.

Afterward, as Grace lay in the darkened room, her head resting on Luke's chest, she said, "We can't just let it end now, can we?"

He put his hand on her head and twined his fingers through her hair. "It'll never end, Grace. It began twenty years ago, and you still own me. But if we keep doing this, it's only going to get harder to say good-bye."

Tears pricked her eyes. She knew he was right. "This seems to be our lot, doesn't it? Something always comes between us."

He was silent a long moment, then said, "Maybe someday the way will be clear."

He didn't believe it any more than she did, she knew. She couldn't imagine him moving to New Jersey, giving up the life he'd created here. Even this house had taken him years to build; he wasn't going to give that up.

And she'd never ask him to.

"I only wish we'd done the right thing all those years ago."

"We did, Grace." He touched her cheek and smiled a little sadly. "We did the right thing."

"How can you say that?"

"Because you needed to stretch your wings. You *needed* to get out of Blue Moon Bay and see what life was like in the big world. If you hadn't, you would have been dissatisfied forever. But I couldn't do that with you. If we'd had a relationship back then, it would have held you back, and we would have resented each other.''

"You're right,'' she said, her voice catching in her throat. "You're right.''

The minutes stretched long as they lay in the dark.

Finally, it was Grace who spoke. "I guess now we're going to have to work together and somehow pretend this didn't happen.''

"We have some experience with that.''

"Yes, we do. You'd think by now we'd be used to it.''

"Maybe we are. Look, we don't have to work together. The only time we even have to be in the same room is at the silent auction. After that, there's nothing until Christmas. I'm sure we'll have forgotten all about this by then.'' He laughed quietly.

"Right. So all we have to do is get past the auction, and it's smooth sailing.''

"Nothin' to it.''

"Then why haven't the past seventeen years and four hundred miles done the trick?''

"Because we had questions. Unanswered questions. Now they're answered.''

"Ah. So I guess we should stop asking them.''

"We should *definitely* stop asking them.''

"You're right. I know you're right.''

Luke took a long breath then said, "Look, there's something else I need to tell you. I spoke with Fred Bailey, and he agrees there should be a reward for finding that jewelry. If it turns out that it *does* belong to the school as part of Edna's estate, that reward will go to you and Jimmy.''

"Reward? As in *financial* reward?''

He nodded. "Fred was thinking maybe five percent of the eventual sale price."

Grace did some quick calculations based on Vernon Shepherd's previous appraisal, then gasped and looked up at him. "But that would be—"

"Enough to help you move back north," Luke finished. He let out a long breath. "You could go."

"You arranged that for me? Knowing that was what I'd do with it?"

"Of course. I don't want you to go, Grace, but I'm not going to trick you into staying. I would never get in the way of what you wanted. Or what you need."

She laid her head back down on his chest. "Thank you, Luke," she said softly. Then, trying not to cry, she closed her eyes and listened to his heartbeat until she fell asleep with his words ringing in her heart.

You still own me.

Chapter Fourteen

The Connor School Thirty-First Annual Silent Auction and Ball, held at the Dolittle Mansion on the outskirts of town, had begun at 8:00 p.m.

By 8:10 p.m., Grace wanted to leave.

It wasn't that the dance wasn't wonderful. It was. She hadn't been to the Dolittle Mansion since she was a child, but it was every bit as magnificent as she'd remembered. Maybe even more magnificent, because now she got to wear a beautiful strapless red gown and sip bubbly champagne from tall flutes.

In a way, she felt just like Cinderella.

The problem was Prince Charming. Or, in this case, Luke Stewart. Ever since their night together two and a half weeks ago, she hadn't been able to stop thinking about him. They had only made love twice, but in her mind she had relived it a hundred times. Every night when she lay in bed she replayed each and every detail.

She wanted to see him again, to spend every night with him until she had to leave. But they'd agreed that they were going to end things before they started.

So they'd steadfastly avoided each other at work, with the hopes that they'd satiated their lingering lust for each other and they could now get on with their lives. The hope had been that, with the question "What would it be like?" answered, the desire would be gone.

It wasn't. Not for Grace, anyway. Although she'd busied herself with press releases and publicity for the auction—efforts which had resulted in the sale of an extra three hundred tickets—her mind had drifted constantly back to Luke.

Just as her eyes did tonight.

He looked incredible in a black tux that seemed as if it had been made just for him. Every time she glanced his way, which was pretty often, she felt her heart slam into her throat—particularly since he was usually glancing in her direction at the same time.

Part of her wondered what was the harm in having a fling for as long as they could. But she knew the answer, at least for herself. Her feelings went beyond lust and way beyond curiosity. She was falling hard for Luke. And she wasn't sure she could bear the pain of giving him up when it was time to leave.

"Champagne, miss?" a waiter asked, extending a silver tray of champagne flutes out to her.

"Thank you," she said, taking one. She didn't really want it, but at least it provided a moment's diversion. She'd give the drink to her mother when she saw her.

"Enjoying yourself?" an achingly familiar voice said behind her. She felt him touch her elbow lightly before she turned to face him.

"Oh, Luke, there you are."

"And here you are. Want to slip out back?"

Her face grew warm. "You know we can't do that."

"I know. But do you *want* to?"

"No."

"Liar."

Another waiter approached them, and she set the champagne glass down on his tray.

"Want to keep your wits about you, huh?" Luke asked. "I don't blame you."

"Have you seen my mother anywhere?" Grace asked, deliberately changing the subject. "It's not like her to be late like this."

Luke shook his head. "Fred isn't here yet either. Maybe there's some kind of traffic tie-up because of the interest in this auction."

"Fred's not here?" Grace repeated. "That's quite a coincidence. You know, my mom was supposed to introduce me to her mystery man tonight. You don't suppose…? No, no way."

"What, that your mom and Fred are seeing each other? Why not?"

"They've known each other for years! Nothing ever happened before."

Luke gave her a look. "Nothing's impossible."

She sighed, looking into his eyes. "I wish that were true."

"It is." He smiled and pointed toward the doorway.

There, dressed to the nines, were Fred Bailey and Dot Perigon, arm-in-arm. Dot waved at Grace when she saw her and came over, Fred at her elbow.

"Honey, you look beautiful," she said, beaming at Grace.

"So do you," Grace returned. "But…Mr. Bailey…is he the one…?"

Fred chuckled and patted Dot's arm. "I certainly hope I am." He turned his attention to Luke and said, "For fifty years, I've pined for this woman. Ever since she dumped me for this lovely lady's father in high school. And now, I believe I have finally won her over."

"Perseverance pays off," Luke said with a laugh, shooting another meaningful look at Grace. "Congratulations."

"No congratulations are due yet," Fred said, with a lift of his brow. "But in the future…who knows?"

Grace watched in astonishment. She couldn't have imagined a more perfect match for her mother, apart from her father. If she'd had any doubts about the suitability of the match, the glow in her mother's eyes erased them. She was happy. She looked more alive than she had in ten years.

Maybe she was even in love.

"I'm really happy for you, Mom," Grace said, giving her mother a hug. "This is wonderful news."

The band began to play "Moonlight Serenade" and Fred turned to Dot. "I think they're playing our song."

"This was never our song, you old dear." Dot laughed. "We're not *that* old."

"When you're around, my dear, *any* song is our song." He put a strong, steady hand out to her. "May I have this dance?"

"Certainly!" She was like a girl again, laughing.

Fred smiled at Luke and Grace. "Please excuse us."

Luke nodded.

Grace watched as he led her mother to the dance floor and they began to dance slowly, perfectly in sync, like a couple who had been together for years and years. In a way, she supposed, they had been. The friendship they'd shared was a rock-solid foundation for whatever the future held for them.

She suspected that her father would approve.

"It's good to see her so happy," Grace said to Luke, a bit wistfully.

"It would be good to see you happy, too."

"I'm fine."

"Fine." He laughed. "You always hated that word."

Yes, she had. And she hated characterizing her life that way too. "You don't miss a thing, do you?"

"I've missed plenty in my life," he said, cocking his head fractionally as he looked at her. "Plenty."

Her chest tightened. "You're not alone."

"Yes, Grace," he said, with a short, humorless laugh. "I am."

That assertion made her feel both sad and relieved. She wanted to reach out to the loner in him, to hold him and love him and make everything all right for him. But she couldn't do that. And knowing she couldn't, some small, jealous part of her preferred that no other woman did either.

More than anything, though, she wanted him to be happy. She truly did. "You're not going to be alone for long," she said. "Guy like you? No way."

"I don't know. Now that ol' Fred's finally having a little romance, someone has to take the reins as the town's resident bachelor. Town's gotta have a resident bachelor."

"You're not like Fred."

"Are you sure?"

She shook her head. "I can't quite see you spending the next forty years alone with your work. Someone's going to lasso you sooner or later. Have you noticed some of the predatory looks the women here are giving you?''

A faint flush came into his cheeks. ''Oh, come on, Grace.''

''I'm serious, Luke, mascara'd eyes are batting at you wherever you go. The single-female population of Blue Moon Bay must be throwing themselves at you daily.'' She hated the idea but was certain she was correct. ''Frankly, I don't know how you've stayed single this long.''

He looked at her, his ice-blue eyes tinged with warmth. ''It's not so easy to find someone you're willing to spend the rest of your life with.''

She gave a dry laugh. ''Marriage isn't necessarily a lifetime commitment.''

''For me it would be,'' he said softly.

''It should be.''

He shrugged. ''Which is why it hasn't happened.''

''I guess you just haven't met the right girl yet, then.'' She held her breath as she waited for his response.

He gazed at some far-off spot across the room. ''I don't know.''

Something in her deflated. But what had she expected? A vehement, though mournful, proclamation of his love and devotion, even though she'd made it clear that she wasn't sticking around for it?

''Wouldn't matter that much if I had,'' he continued, turning his gaze to her. ''It's not just about finding the right person, it's about finding the right person at the right time.'' A beat passed. ''Isn't it?''

''Yes, I suppose it is.'' Then she asked, tentatively, ''Do you think there's more than one right person?''

She wasn't positive she wanted to hear the answer, but curiosity drove her to ask.

A moment later, she was positive she *didn't* want to hear the answer. Judy Flynn slunk up so quietly that Grace jumped when she heard her voice from behind.

"Hey, Luke, lookin' good." She brushed past Grace, a trail of Obsession perfume wafting behind her, and went straight to Luke. She curled her arm around his and kissed his cheek, leaving a hot-pink smudge behind. "Oh, hey, Grace," she said, pressing, if possible, even closer to Luke. "Wow, I don't think I've ever seen you in a dress."

Grace didn't know what to say to that, although a lot of inappropriate responses came to mind. "I do have one or two of them," she said curtly. "Though I find they're not that easy to drive in."

Judy burst into a shrill giggle. "Can you *imagine* that? What a funny picture that puts in my head."

Grace sighed heavily and glanced at Luke, who, she was glad to see, was trying to disentangle his arm from Judy's.

"I'll bet most of the parents here won't even recognize you in that get-up," Judy continued.

"She looks beautiful," Luke said, holding Grace's gaze with his own. "She always looks beautiful."

A thrill tickled across Grace's skin.

"Oh, she is, she's just as cute as a button," Judy said, a little too enthusiastically. She gave Luke's arm a squeeze. "I'm with you on that one."

"I'd better go check on Jimmy," Grace said, eager to get away from the sight of Judy hanging on Luke. If they weren't having an affair now, she was pretty sure they had in the past. Or might in the future. Or both. Judy was awfully familiar with him.

"Bye-bye!" Judy trilled.

"Grace," Luke said, breaking free of Judy's tenacious grasp.

She stopped and turned to face him. "Yes?"

The band launched into "Autumn Leaves."

"You promised me a dance, remember?" He didn't give her a chance to object, but took her hand in his and said over his shoulder to Judy, "Excuse us, Jude."

Judy thrust her bottom lip out and gave a tiny wave. "I get the next one, Luke," she called.

"She'll be lying in wait for the music to end," Grace commented as he led her onto the dance floor.

"Maybe it won't end," he said, smoothly drawing her close and slipping an arm around her waist.

She was comfortable against him. It felt safe. And just a little dangerous. She could have stayed forever. "Believe me, it'll end." She reached up and rubbed the lipstick smudge off his cheek with her thumb. "And Judy will be waiting."

He clasped her hand in his. "Does that bother you?"

"Of course not! You can do whatever you want."

"No. No, I can't."

"Why not? You're a grown man."

"That doesn't mean I can do whatever I want to do."

She raised an eyebrow. "What is it you want to do?"

He smiled and pulled her closer. "Well, now, I'm not so sure you want to know the answer to that, as it does involve you."

Her heartbeat accelerated against his chest. "Then, in that case, I *definitely* want to know."

He adjusted his arm around her waist and drew her close enough to whisper in her ear. "What I want to do is take you out of here, find a secluded spot on the beach and peel that dress off you.''

Her breath caught in her throat. "Then what?" she asked, her voice barely a whisper.

"Then…" His words were hot against her neck. "I want to shake your hair out of that old-lady bun you've got it in."

"Hey," she objected half-heartedly. "It took me hours to make this *chignon.*"

"And it would take about two seconds to take it out."

Suddenly, the chignon felt tight, along with every muscle in her body. And she'd love nothing more than to let Luke loosen her up. "Then what would you do?"

"You want the short answer or the long one?"

She closed her eyes and leaned her head against him. "Oh, the long one. Absolutely."

He laughed softly against her hair. "Those shoes…"

"My Stephinios?" Her pair of Italian black-leather Dario Stephinios was one of the only luxury items she hadn't sold at a yard sale after the divorce. They had impossibly high heels and made her feet hurt but they made her legs look great. Or at least she thought she did. "You don't like them?"

"They can stay," he said. "They make your legs look great. Not that your legs need any help in that department."

Her skin tingled all over. He was batting a thousand with her. "If I'm not mistaken, you're completely dressed in this scenario and I'm naked but for my four-inch-high heels."

He drew back for a moment and gave her a rakish smile. "Now that you mention it, this penguin suit *is* beginning to feel…stifling."

She laughed. "I could help you with that."

"I wish you would."

"Imagine it done," she said, doing just that. "What happens next?"

"We're all alone in a secluded cove on the beach with nothing but our shoes on—"

"*Our* shoes?" Grace interrupted. "You mean you left yours on too?"

He nodded solemnly. "And the socks. The shoes are uncomfortable without the socks."

She gave a shriek of laughter, drawing the glances of couples dancing nearby.

"You're going to get us in trouble," he said softly, turning her to a more private corner of the dance floor.

"Okay, okay, I'm sorry." She sobered up. "What's next? Tell me more."

"You're a big girl now, Grace. What do you think happens next?"

A thousand delectable possibilities came to mind. Suddenly, things didn't seem so funny anymore.

"Tell me," she said, wishing desperately that they could go outside where he could *show* her.

He bent close to her ear and said, "Next I'd make love to you all night long."

She swallowed hard. "All night?"

He nodded. "And in the morning, we'd get up and do it again. We've got a lot of time to make up for. Both the past and the future."

"Sounds like more than one night and one morning's worth."

"I could keep going."

"No doubt. That's quite a scenario you've come up with there, Mr. Stewart."

"You haven't heard the half of it."

"Really?" Her mouth felt dry. If he kept talking like this, she was going to lose control of herself and attack him right here in the middle of the dance floor. She groaned in frustration. "We shouldn't be talking like this, Luke. Truly. It can't go anywhere. All it will do is make us crazy."

"I know it." He took her hand and, with a surreptitious glance around, raised it to his lips.

She leaned her forehead against their hands for a moment, then looked into his eyes. "How are we going to get through the rest of the year like this?"

"Lots of cold showers, I guess. Alone."

"That doesn't work."

"It's the best I can do." He tightened his grasp on her hand. "I thought I could get you out of my system, Grace, but I don't think it's possible. This isn't just lust or curiosity. You're in my heart."

Her knees felt weak, and she leaned closer to him for support. "Please don't say that, Luke."

"It's true." He twined his fingers through hers. "It's been true for years."

"But there's nothing we can do about it."

"Well, you could always reconsider and stay."

A lump grew in her throat. She wanted nothing more than to do just that. "No, I can't. You know that. What *I* want—even what *we* want—doesn't matter right now. My first responsibility is to my child."

"Maybe you could make him understand, maybe he'd agree to stay."

"Oh, I'm sure he would," Grace said sadly. "Jimmy's a good kid. I could tell him we were staying and that was that, and he probably wouldn't even argue. But he'd be miserable, and he'd keep it all inside." She shook her head. "You know, I took him to a child psychologist last year when all of this began, because he started having anxiety attacks. Can you imagine? Nine years old and the kid's already having anxiety attacks!''

''What did the doctor say?''

Grace shrugged. ''That Jimmy keeps a lot of stuff inside. I try to draw him out as much as I can, but he's so eager to say what he thinks I want to hear, that half the time I'm not sure whether to believe him or not. So he tells me everything's fine and I believe it—then the next thing I know, he's trading jewelry to kids for the junk food in their lunches.''

Luke held her close. ''You don't think that's just normal for a kid? Wanting sugary treats?''

''I don't know. Plenty of kids gave the sugary treats up for trinkets, didn't they?''

''Sometimes kids just want stuff they don't already have. It doesn't have to be such a bad thing.''

''Well, I hope it isn't, but I'm not willing to take the chance. I promised him we'd go back to New Jersey. Before we left, he told me that was what he wanted more than anything, and I promised I'd do it for him. So I'm going to.''

A moment passed before Luke said, ''I don't know how Michael ended up with someone like you.''

She laughed. ''I don't think he knew what he was getting into. We were kids. We didn't *really* know each other. We didn't even know ourselves. You were smart to do things the way you did.''

''I don't know. If things had been just a little different, maybe I would have done exactly what Michael did.''

She gave a derisive snort. ''What, moved away, start a family, then leave them?''

"No, Grace, that's not what I meant." The music ended and they pulled apart as everyone clapped for the band.

Fred Bailey called out the name of another old standard, and the band launched into it, with Fred and Dot leading the crowd on the dance floor.

"Look at them, would you?" Luke said, gesturing at the older couple. "He had a long wait, but he finally got the grand prize."

"It was an *awfully* long wait," Grace agreed, wondering if anyone—if Luke—would wait that long for her, and how on earth she could make it worth it if he did. "Most people wouldn't wait so long."

"No, they wouldn't." Luke took two champagne glasses off the tray from a passing waiter. "I can only guess that he never met anyone else who compared to her, and he didn't want to settle for less." He handed Grace a glass.

She took it and looked at him. "I'm beginning to understand that."

"Me too."

They clinked their glasses together and sipped.

It was on the tip of Grace's tongue to ask Luke again if he'd ever consider moving to New Jersey, but she knew the answer. Luke Stewart would be a fish out of water in New Jersey. Even if he would go, which she doubted, he'd be desperate to leave. It was clear that he'd found his life here in Blue Moon Bay. The kids at the school adored him, and he was wonderful with them. It wouldn't be fair to anyone to take him away from that.

They both knew it.

"I hope Jimmy's having a good time," Grace said, in an effort to change the hopeless course of her thoughts. "There aren't as many kids here as I thought there would be."

"It's hard to compete with video games these days," Luke agreed. "But he's a sport. I'm sure he's all right. You want me to check?"

She considered his offer briefly—thinking about how Michael always expected her to take care of anything child-related herself—then shook her head. "No, it would probably just embarrass him to have one of us going in to check up on him. I'm sure he's fine."

"Luke," Judy's sing-songy voice called from several yards away. She came tripping over to them, empty champagne glass in hand. "You said you'd save a dance for me."

He flashed Grace an exasperated look, then said, "How about we get you some coffee, Judy?"

She giggled. "Whatever you think, Luke."

"Care to join us?" he asked Grace doubtfully. "It shouldn't take long."

She shook her head. "No, thanks. I'll wait here." *At least for now.*

She watched him walk away with Judy and sighed. She had no right to feel jealous. She had no claim on Luke. She never had and she never would.

She just had to get used to that.

Jimmy was miserable.

Why his mother had made him come to this stupid ball or auction or *whatever* it was, he didn't know. After all, he could have gone to stay with Jenna. He liked playing with her kids, even if they were a couple of years younger than he was and one of them was a girl. They were fun. He could have been running around Jenna's large yard right now, playing ghost in the graveyard and freeze tag, but no, he had to come to the Dolittle Mansion to this fancy dance that looked like something from Cinderella or something. Worse, the only two kids his age were Melanie Price and Dale Weingarten. He didn't want to talk to either one of them.

"Grandma has been coming to this dance every year for thirty years," his mother had told him. "It must be fun."

"Fun for an old lady," he'd pointed out.

You would have thought he'd called his *mom* an old lady. "James Alexander Bowes, you watch that attitude." Then she looked guilty and added, "You know, it's thanks to you that this is going to be such a big deal this year. You found the jewels and probably saved the school from ruin."

There was nothing he could do but shrug at that. Because he didn't want to admit that ever since Buddy Reese had backed off, he'd had a lot more friends and was actually coming to like the Connor School. He didn't want it to close.

But he could never admit he liked school.

"I didn't do anything," he said. "I just found some things and traded them for desserts at lunchtime. Last time I did that, you got mad at me."

"Well, make no mistake, I don't like it when you give kids stuff in exchange for sugary desserts, and I *don't* want you to do it again. But in this case, you really came out a hero."

A *hero*. He liked that.

"So this year there's a children's dance during the adult function," his mom went on. "You'll probably see a bunch of your friends from school, and everyone's going to think you're the coolest guy for finding that stuff. It'll be fun.''

He knew he was in trouble then. Those were her Famous Last Words. *It'll be fun.* That's what she'd said about Camp Winnatuck, where he'd nearly drowned when his inner tube popped in the lake. She'd also said it would be fun to go miniature golfing last week, and then some guy's red ''hole in one'' ball came flying over the pirate and hit Jimmy in the shoulder.

Jimmy was starting to think that when his mother said *It'll be fun,* he should run and hide until the ''fun'' passed.

Sitting in a nearly empty room with a couple of stupid girls and some boring teenage baby-sitters was *not* fun.

The teenagers were talking about boys they liked. Jimmy rolled his eyes and went to the snack table. The punch wasn't bad, so he had two cups of that and stuffed some Oreos into his pockets. He started to leave the table, then went back for a few more cookies. He had a lot of time to kill.

He wished he'd been allowed to stay at Jenna's. Her husband, Bob, had talked about taking the kids fishing in the evening. *Fishing!* Most of the fish Jimmy had seen in his life had been on shaved ice in glass cabinets at the grocery store. Or they were in big tanks that people told him not to tap on.

He hoped they were going to stay in Blue Moon Bay at least long enough for him to go fishing a time or two. And boating. And trick-or-treating in the center of town, where Kevin Dogherty had said the shopkeepers all gave out buckets of candy.

He sighed. There was a lot of stuff he wanted to do here. Suddenly, a year didn't seem so long at all.

He started to go back to the folding chair he'd been sitting on for the past half hour, but he couldn't stand the idea of listening to all those girls anymore. So, after a quick glance to make sure the baby-sitters weren't looking, he slipped out into the hallway.

Just the fact that he wasn't really supposed to be there made things a little more interesting. Not that anyone had said he wasn't *allowed* to go in the hall— he'd totally learned his lesson when it came to going to places that were off limits. But this was just a little more interesting than sitting around eating cookies and ignoring Melanie and Dale.

He walked down the hallway, looking at all the decorations someone had put up. There were silver stars hanging from the ceiling and crepe-paper streamers stuck like spaghetti to the beams overhead.

As he was rounding the corner, he saw, and heard, two thin women in glittery dresses, one with blond hair and one with hair so red it looked purple, talking about his mother.

"...poor Grace never even knew. Lord spare me the fate of having a husband like Michael Bowes. He may be good-looking, but he's bad through and through. And he's got no conscience about it whatsoever."

Jimmy stepped back and flattened himself against the wall, listening to their conversation on the other side.

"Don't I know it," the other woman responded. "You know, Michael was the one who broke up the Hessmans' marriage. *And,* ironically, he's the one who stole Sam Hessman's car in high school. Remember that?"

The blonde clapped a hand to her smiling red mouth. "No! Everyone thought Luke was behind that."

"Oh, don't get me started on Luke. The things he

let people think about him…of course, it did lend to that deliciously racy reputation he had, which made *all* the girls want him. Myself included, I'll admit it.''

''You're not alone,'' the blonde agreed, clicking her tongue against her teeth. ''But he's always had eyes for just one woman.''

They looked at each other knowingly and said, at the same time, ''Grace.''

''Too bad she stayed with that good-for-nothing Michael Bowes.''

Another voice joined them, saying, ''Michael Bowes? Mean as a snake.''

''You got bitten too, huh?'' one of the women asked.

The new voice laughed and said, ''Literally and figuratively.''

Jimmy couldn't listen to any more. He knew his father could be mean, that wasn't news, but he *bit* people? And stole cars? And broke things? On *purpose?*

If everyone thought that about his dad, what must they think about him? No wonder Buddy Reese had been so mean! He probably thought Jimmy was just like his father.

Was he?

Would he grow up to be the same?

No longer caring if anyone saw him or not, Jimmy ran out the front door and into the night. He didn't know where he was going. He only knew he had to get away from the Dolittle Mansion, and from everyone who knew his father and said bad things about him.

Luke returned to Grace soon after taking Judy for coffee. She had, he explained, decided she wanted to lie down for a few moments on the sofa in the ladies' room.

The band finished playing "If Ever I Would Leave You" and announced they were taking a break. Fred and Dot came over to Luke and Grace, their faces flushed pink from dancing.

"This evening is already a rousing success," Fred said to Grace. "It was a brilliant idea you had, Grace, selling the jewels like this. I've seen some of the bids, and they've far exceeded our expectations."

Grace smiled. "That's wonderful."

"And it's thanks to you," Luke said.

"Um, Mrs. Bowes?"

They all turned their attention to the lanky teenage girl who had spoken. Grace recognized her as one of the baby-sitters at the children's dance.

"Do you have your son?" the girl asked.

"Do *I* have him?" Grace's heart hammered in her chest immediately. The auction was instantly forgotten. "I thought *you* had him."

The girl kneaded her hands before her. "Well, we did, but then he, like, disappeared."

"How long has he been gone?" Luke asked, his voice hard enough to make the girl wince.

"I don't know. Like, ten minutes?"

He flashed her an angry look and said to Grace, "You check out back, and I'll look in the front by the cars. Fred—"

"Dot and I'll search the mansion," Fred said, in the same confident voice Luke was using. "Don't worry, Gracie, I'm sure Jimmy's just fooling around."

She hoped so. Last time he'd run off, it was because Buddy Reese was threatening him. Maybe something had happened at the dance. It didn't matter at the moment. What mattered was that she find him.

She took her impractical high-heeled shoes off and

threw them aside, racing to the back lawn of the mansion. Half an acre of manicured gardens and short grass, surrounded by a tall brick wall, greeted her eyes. Within about ten minutes, she knew Jimmy wasn't there. She made her way back to the front, checking both side yards with increasing panic. The back and sides were comparatively safe. The front, where Luke was looking, opened to the road.

She shuddered to think of the possibilities, imagining everything from abduction to a miserable Jimmy trying to hitchhike back to New Jersey.

She surveyed the ocean of cars in the parking lot. At first she didn't see anyone at all. Then she saw Luke, standing still in the far lane, near where Grace had parked. He was just standing there, not walking the aisles between the cars or calling out for Jimmy.

She ran toward him, still afraid but now hopeful that his stillness meant that he'd found Jimmy, safe and sound.

As she got closer, she saw Luke was talking, and she slowed down, her feet silent on the warm asphalt of the parking lot. In front of Luke was a smaller figure. Jimmy. Luke leaned with one arm against Grace's car, listening to the boy. She could hear the small sniffles from several yards away.

"...you knew him, right? Is he really a bad guy?"

Luke looked pained in the mellow light of the street lamp. "Your dad has many good qualities," Luke said. "I think what you heard was people who were jealous of your mom and dad because they were so popular here."

Jimmy sniffed again. "But they said he stole cars and things. And that he *bit* people and broke their marriages. They said he didn't have a conscience at all."

Grace noticed a muscle ticking in Luke's jaw, and she knew exactly what he was thinking. Michael had the devil in him, and whatever Jimmy had heard, it probably wasn't half as bad as the truth.

"It's true, your dad and I got into some trouble in high school. I can't deny that. But he wasn't a *bad* person."

"I've never heard anyone say anything good about him except my mom, and when she does, I can tell it's because she feels like she *has* to."

Grace bit her knuckle. She thought she'd done a good job of hiding her true feelings about Michael, but it seemed Jimmy wasn't buying into it.

"I'll tell you a story about your dad," Luke said, after a moment. "When we were kids, we got a hold of some fireworks. Roman candles, do you know what those are?"

Jimmy nodded eagerly. "He got those every Fourth of July. It was a secret." His small shoulders rose and fell. "He never let me touch them."

"Well, that's good. See, we were shooting them off, and I got this dumb idea that we should shoot them into the trees to scare the birds so they'd all come flying out at once."

"Why?"

Luke shrugged. "It was a really dumb idea, and I'd *never* do it again. Anyway, I was shooting the Roman candles into the trees when your dad noticed a dog on the other side, right in the line of fire, so you know what he did?"

Jimmy shook his blond head.

"He grabbed the burning firework and ground it into the dirt so it wouldn't hurt the dog. It hurt his hand, but the dog was okay."

"Really?" Jimmy smiled and sniffed. "My dad did that?"

Luke nodded. "He did. Now, you may hear that story while you're here, and people may have the details mixed up, but now you know what *really* happened. It's the same with anything else you might hear. That's how gossip works. A story gets going, and no one really cares about getting the details right."

Jimmy nodded.

"So no one really knows your mom and dad except them. And you. So if you hear people talking, it's probably just because people love to gossip. And it's a lot more interesting to some folks to say something bad about a person than to say something good. Got it?"

"Yeah. I guess."

"So are you okay?"

"I'm okay. I just…"

"What?"

"I wish we were staying here."

"What do you mean?"

"My mom and me. I wish we could stay here instead of moving *again.* I don't want to go back to New Jersey."

Luke looked surprised. "You don't?"

Jimmy gave an exaggerated shrug and heaved a sigh. "My mom wants to go back, so I tell her I want to go, too, but I think I like it better here. Not *here,* like at this dance, but here in Blue Moon Bay."

"No kidding," Luke said, nodding slowly. He was smiling. "I'm glad to hear that, because I sure want you to stay. We'll have to talk about that some more, for sure, but right now we've got to hurry up and find your mom, because I know she's worried sick about you."

"I'm here," Grace said, stepping quickly out of the shadows as if she'd just run down the lawn. She didn't want Jimmy to know she'd heard them talking about Michael. She wanted him to feel he had an adult confidant, even if it wasn't her. Somehow she'd have to find another way to raise the subject of staying in Blue Moon Bay.

"Jimmy, what are you doing out here?" she asked, trying to sound stern but falling short.

"We were just having a talk," Luke answered, putting a protective hand on Jimmy's shoulder.

"You scared me to death." Grace extended her arms, and her son ran into them. She buried her face in his hair for a moment, gave him an extra squeeze, then said, "Grandma and Mr. Bailey are inside looking for you. I want you to go in and get one of the babysitters to help you find them and tell them you're back, okay? I want to talk to Luke for a moment."

"All right," Jimmy said, and with one furtive glance at Luke, he took off for the front door of the mansion.

Grace watched him go until he was inside, then turned to Luke with a heart that felt like one of Dali's melting clocks.

"Good story," she said. "Too bad it was Michael who was trying to hit that dog—" she reached over and took Luke's hand, turning it to reveal a scar near his wrist "—and you who burned the hell out of your hand trying to stop it." She ran a finger across the scar, then raised his hand to her lips and kissed it.

"He wants to stay," Luke said softly.

"I heard that," she said, hardly daring to hope, holding fast to his hand.

"So, ah, you think you might stick around for a while after all?"

She smiled. She couldn't stop it. "Maybe. I do have a job I can't just abandon."

"That's right. As you know, it's not easy to find someone to fill that position."

"Of course, I'd need a raise," she said, cocking an eyebrow. "And maybe some other perks to tempt me to stay."

"Darlin', you can have whatever perks you want. Hell, I'll even include room and board in your salary."

She laughed and ran her fingertips down his lapels. "That the best you can do?"

"Oh, no," he said, a sly smile playing at his mouth. "Come home with me tonight, and I'll show you the best I can do."

Her breathing grew shallow. "Could be a long night."

"I hope so," he said, and pulled her into his arms.

Epilogue

A month after the ball, they were sitting on the porch swing on Grace's mother's veranda. The harvest moon shone overhead like a great big night-light, casting a silvery glow over the landscape and throwing tall shadows from the trees onto the lawn.

"I have something for you," Luke said. He seemed nervous. It might have been her imagination, but he was talking a little faster than normal, and when he took her hands his appeared to be shaking.

Maybe he'd just had coffee with dinner and it was the caffeine.

Luke had been in meetings all day with financial advisers and the board of directors, but he'd called her late in the morning to arrange to see her. He said it was important, and that he wanted her to wait up even though he couldn't get there before about ten o'clock.

Staying up was easy. Waiting, however, was more

difficult. Grace wondered all day what he had to say to her, especially on the heels of an all-day board extravaganza. Was it good news…like she was getting a raise?

Or bad…like she was fired?

Did he have an actual pink slip to give her?

"What's going on, Luke?" she asked. "Is this good or bad?"

"It's good. I mean, I hope you'll think it's good." He cleared his throat and reached into his pocket.

Grace's breath caught in her throat.

He pulled out a small black velvet box. "This is for you. I hope you'll accept it."

This wasn't happening. This couldn't be happening. She hadn't expected it at all, yet nothing had ever come as a more welcome surprise. "Luke, is this…?" She took the box and opened it.

But when she looked in, she nearly started in surprise. Then she gave a shout of laughter. The cardboard insert had been taken out of the box to make the inside roomy enough to hold a gleaming silver key. "Now I *really* don't know what to say. What is this?"

"Come and see," he said, standing up and leading her off the porch. They stepped down into the darkness of the front yard, and Grace realized that Luke's car wasn't parked in the usual spot on the driveway.

"Where did you park?"

"Shh!" He led her around the side of the house and stood back. "Voilà!"

There, under the light of her father's shed, was a brand-new shining yellow school bus.

She looked at it wryly and chuckled. "I guess I'm not fired, then."

"Why would you be fired? You're the best bus driver we've ever had. Apart from me, that is."

She smiled and shook her head. "High praise indeed." A tiny disappointment wormed its way around her stomach, but she tried not to let it show. "Wow. Too bad Jimmy's already asleep. This is something."

"Got it today," Luke said proudly. "As you can see, we haven't even had time to have the school name painted on the side."

"It's…great."

"You bet it is. It even has air-conditioning." He led her to the door. "Go inside. Check it out."

She opened the door and climbed aboard, with Luke close behind. The interior smelled of new vinyl. She had to admit, the bus *was* awfully nice. She sat in the driver's seat. It was springy and comfortable.

"Should we go for a spin?" she asked.

"Go for it."

She put the key in the ignition and was about to start it, when a glimmer, in midair, about a foot away from her, caught her eye. "What the…?" She turned on the inside light.

And her jaw dropped.

Hanging from the rearview mirror, dangling on the end of a length of fishing line, was the ring she'd admired from Edna Connor's collection. The ring that had belonged to Princess Mirabelle.

The *engagement* ring of Princess Mirabelle.

Unable to form any words, she looked at Luke and questioned him with eyes that burned.

"It's just until I can find some fuzzy dice." He smiled and gave a quick shrug.

"Luke…" Tears spilled onto her cheeks.

"Oh, no, don't cry." He knelt in front of her, cupped

her face in his hands, and brushed the tears away with his thumbs. "Don't cry," he repeated softly, kissing her lips.

"What does this mean?" she asked.

"It means I want to marry you and spend the rest of my life with you," he said, taking her hands in his. "I realize you may be cautious about this right now. Hell, I've been cautious about it for too many years. But I let you get away once, and I've kicked myself for seventeen years for not trying to stop you, so I can't make that mistake again."

"Oh, Luke." She laid a hand against his cheek. "Are you sure you want this?"

"I want what you want, Grace. It became so clear to me when we talked that night. I want kids, and Christmas mornings and homemade Halloween costumes. I want to grow old with you and spend my retirement money on bingo at the fire hall. But more than anything, I want to go to sleep with you every night and wake up by your side every morning."

She smiled. "That's what I want too."

He kissed her. "I love you, Grace. There will never be another woman for me." He kissed her hands: one, then the other.

"What do you say?"

"I say yes." As she answered, she realized that she felt the same. Exactly the same. That this was perhaps the first time she'd ever been so sure about anything. "I love you too, Luke, and yes, I'll marry you."

* * * * *

▼ SILHOUETTE®
SPECIAL EDITION™

AVAILABLE FROM 15TH AUGUST 2003

THE HEART BENEATH Lindsay McKenna

Morgan's Mercenaries

As Lieutenant Wes James and Lieutenant Callie Evans raced to save victims in an earthquake-ravaged city, past pain kept Wes from surrendering his heart. But he ached to make Callie his…

MAC'S BEDSIDE MANNER Marie Ferrarella

Blair Memorial

Dr Harrison MacKenzie wasn't used to women resisting him—but feisty nurse Jolene DeLuca's flashing green eyes told him to keep away. He was captivated…but could he convince her to trust him?

HER BACHELOR CHALLENGE
Cathy Gillen Thacker

The Deveraux Legacy

Businesswoman Bridgett Owens wanted to settle down—but irresistible bachelor Chase Deveraux was not the sort of man she wanted to marry. Until a passionate encounter changed everything…

THE COYOTE'S CRY Jackie Merritt

The Coltons

Falling for off-limits beauty Jenna Elliot was Bram Colton's worst nightmare—and ultimate fantasy. But now that she was sharing his home, he couldn't ignore the intense passion between them…

THE BOSS'S BABY BARGAIN Karen Sandler

Lucas Taylor only married his secretary Allie so that he'd be able to adopt a child—but a night of passion resulted in pregnancy. Could he overcome his past and keep the love he'd always longed for?

HIS ARCH ENEMY'S DAUGHTER Crystal Green

Kane's Crossing

Rebellious Ashlyn Spencer was the daughter of Sam Reno's worst enemy…yet she melted Sam's defences. Could the brooding sheriff forget her family's crimes and think of a future with her?

Maitland Maternity

Where the luckiest babies are born!

For the Sake of a Child
by Stella Bagwell

A marriage on the brink... A little boy in need...
A family in the making?

Drake Logan was a risk-taker, but not when it came
to his wife's life! He has never stopped missing
Hope. But he is sure he is right, that they
shouldn't have children. Even though she is just as
sure he is wrong!

Hope Logan is delighted that
Drake is coming home for his
little nephew's short visit. The
little boy adores him and she is
hoping it might at least give
them a chance to talk about
the baby issue. But talking is
not all they end up doing and
their temporary reunion
could have unexpected
consequences...

4 Books
and a surprise gift!

We would like to take this opportunity to thank you for reading this Silhouette® book by offering you the chance to take FOUR more specially selected titles from the Special Edition™ series absolutely FREE! We're also making this offer to introduce you to the benefits of the Reader Service™ —

- ★ FREE home delivery
- ★ FREE gifts and competitions
- ★ FREE monthly Newsletter
- ★ Books available before they're in the shops
- ★ Exclusive Reader Service discount

Accepting these FREE books and gift places you under no obligation to buy; you may cancel at any time, even after receiving your free shipment. Simply complete your details below and return the entire page to the address below. **You don't even need a stamp!**

YES! Please send me 4 free Special Edition books and a surprise gift. I understand that unless you hear from me, I will receive 6 superb new titles every month for just £2.90 each, postage and packing free. I am under no obligation to purchase any books and may cancel my subscription at any time. The free books and gift will be mine to keep in any case.

E3ZEF

Ms/Mrs/Miss/Mr ....Initials.................................
BLOCK CAPITALS PLEASE

Surname...

Address...

....

....Postcode ....

Send this whole page to:
UK: The Reader Service, FREEPOST CN81, Croydon, CR9 3WZ
EIRE: The Reader Service, PO Box 4546, Kilcock, County Kildare (stamp required)